Praise For Ted's Secret Dream

For those of us who grew up in rural Texas at about any certain time, the idea of owning a horse was quite a common dream.

Ted's Secret Dream colloquially paints a picture, not just of the early 1940's, which is the setting of the story, that transcends time for us all.

The language the author uses is quite "South Central Texas", and gives the story a realistic "feel"...something like Mark Twain might have done had he lived in the Lone Star State 50 years later.

The book brings to mind (loosely) the theme of the 1950's TV show "Fury", where a young boy around the central character Ted's age (12) befriends and tames a wild stallion. Peter Graves later of "Mission Impossible" fame played the father.

So if you want to go back in your own special time, and join Ted's dream of owing a majestic horse, while enjoying real, honest Texan phraseology and dialog that is etched on the pages like carved leather; you'll want to pick up Ted's Secret Dream.

As the announcer used to say on another TV show around the same era involving a Texan with a certain horse named "Silver", "Now, let us go back to yesteryear"!

Dr. Jerome R. Wilkerson, ND
Austin, Texas

Henry Petru has done a masterful job of capturing the whimsical mind of a Texas teenage boy growing up on a farm in the 40's. No cell phone or computer–just his own imagination to entertain him. As his story unfolds "you'll see it when you believe it" is the life lesson he shares with us all.

Frances Meiser, Author

Henry, standing ovation. Enchanted, page by page, captured tears of joy and bristles of fear. Unexpected conclusion. Excellent read.

Marilou Sacre

Henry Petru's masterful storytelling puts the reader right in the shoes of 12 year old Ted. I was completely drawn into the story and practically could not put the book down until it was done. Each chapter left me wanting to know what would happen next and how the story would be told. The author captured the times and the locale by expertly crafting the dialect, descriptions of people and places and most importantly the feelings.....feelings that only a little boy might have who is yearning deeply for something that seems ephemeral - or is it?

This book is for everyone who can remember or who wants to remember what it is like to go after your deepest desire, to get lost in it, to stay on course, to truly feel your feelings, to live life. Anyone who has been a child can relate to the anticipation, imagination and zeal as a strong desire grows within. I think we can all relate to Ted's adventure one way or another.

Gayla Harris

Ted's Secret Dream

A Tale of Love and Adventure

By Henry Petru

Ted's Secret Dream

A Tale of Love and Adventure

By Henry Petru

Published By

Positive Imaging, LLC

bill@positive-imaging.com

ISBN 9781944071790

Dedication

To Henry, the child within, the young boy who came forth in the early hours, morning after morning, to live and dream a childhood that never was. You and I became friends during this writing and we adventured and explored together. This is your story, not mine. It was you who relived experiences and shared dreams and visions and feelings of a childhood mostly suppressed by the circumstances in which you lived; a childhood that could exist only in the furtive and private chambers of your mind. I harbor the warmest affection for you, dear child, and it is to you—a brilliant, resourceful, brave and sensitive youth—that I dedicate this book.

Contents

1

Discovery

Ted arrived at the lake just as the setting sun was painting the sky orange. The lake, where he enjoyed encounters and fantasies, was his refuge and it always drew him like a magnet. Actually, it was not a lake at all, but a stock tank set at the edge of a forest clearing on the Crockett homestead. Its relatively small size, however, did not prevent everyone from calling it 'The Lake', perhaps to evoke a grander image than was due this body of water that provided drink for the family livestock. For Ted, it truly was a lake and it was his place of fun and dreams.

Ted found his dreaming spot on the bank, a hollow worn smooth by many sittings. Into this depression, he sat down, fixed his gaze into the water and dreamed his dream. From the depths of his mind, as though from the depths of the lake, appeared a horse–his own horse. Ever since he had that dream in 1941 when he was ten years old, Ted wanted his own horse. He dreamed about a spirited animal, a fantasy that had become a passion and a yearning in his heart that screamed to be filled. This passion was satisfied only partly by an old plow horse that lived in the pen by the barn. He was an aging horse that had pulled the plow ahead of his father up and down the rows of the farm for many years. Ted had named him Spectrum. He often rode Spectrum, but the old horse no longer knew the meaning of the command "giddy-up" and had become set in the manner of plodding up and down the field. Riding him was uneventful, mundane and he always returned Spectrum to the pen feeling unsatisfied and unfulfilled.

Settling into the worn spot on the bank, Ted pulled the ever-present harmonica out of his pocket and accompanied his dream with his favorite type of song: a slow, soft, drawnout wailing series of notes as his spirit moved him. He was really playing for himself and it made no difference that no one ever heard him–not the ducks on the lake or the geese in the air; not the rabbits and squirrels in the woods or the fish in the water. But, if only they all understood the beauty and moving experience of his music, they all certainly would have gathered around to hear him play. So sweet and mellow were the sounds.

The cool October breeze enhanced his mood. On the lake, the breeze created wavelets that played with the evening reflections and pushed tiny, sparkling ripples to the shore at Ted's feet. He playfully wiggled his toes into the muddy bank as he breathed out of the harmonica melodies of enticing fantasies. His reverie continued even after he replaced the harmonica back into his pocket. The experience generated a flood of good feelings and, as though propelled by a released spring, he bound up with such a hearty "whoop!" that it shattered the lakeside tranquility. Immediately, from a distance across the lake came a sound like muffled drums.

"Whazzat?" Ted questioned himself under his breath. From across the lake, the drums answered. "Them's hoofbeats!" he declared excitedly. Peering into the waning light of evening, Ted discerned the form of a galloping horse, its hooves pounding up little puffs of dust, its hide reflecting an undulating sheen from the glow of the evening sky. Ted's eyes followed the galloping shadow to the edge of the clearing where it slowed and entered the woods.

Ted stood dumbfounded, marveling for long minutes, unaware that dusk had begun washing the sky of sunset colors and planting ghostly shadows around the lake and in the woods. With pounding hoofbeats echoing in his ears, he finally questioned himself out loud: "Where'd *he* come from?" He knew that no strange horse had ever been seen around the lake, and a domestic animal would not have run. "This must be a wild horse," he mused. The thought sent through his skinny body a pulse of excitement that felt like the horse's kick.

Slowly recovering from the experience, Ted began picturing spellbinding possibilities.

Excitement urged him to hasten home, to tell his father, mother and brother. He began to run toward the house but, after a short distance, he slowed to a fast walk, then to an amble. He considered the ridicule and disbelief he would likely receive when he tried to tell his family about the wild horse. His family seldom believed his stories, and the anticipated disappointment pierced his desire to share his discovery much like the faint shooting star streaking overhead pierced the blackening sky.

Ted decided to keep his secret, to reveal nothing until he gathered more proof.

Determined to see the horse again, he decided that the next morning, Saturday, he would visit the spot where the wild horse had been and would make a plan for observing it. Maybe he would take Spectrum along as a befriending gesture. Maybe he would track down the horse somewhere in the woods. What if he captured it? His mind raced with "maybes" and "what ifs".

As he stepped onto the porch of the house, Ted struggled to contain his excitement. He paused briefly to look back toward the lake as though expecting to see the horse gallop out of the darkness. After lingering just a moment, he turned and slowly entered the house.

"Ted!" his mother called out the moment he closed the door. To Ted, it sounded more like a summons than a greeting and it deflated some of his excitement. Expecting a scolding, he edged his slim body into the living room where the yellow glow of a kerosene lantern hanging from the ceiling revealed his father, Pa Crockett, slouched in his rocker, his huge frame filling the entire seat. Big, club-like hands rested on the arms of the rocker and his head was bent forward slightly as he stared at the floor, a posture that was his custom when he was in thought. At one side, his mother, Ma Crockett, sat in an armless chair, leaning heavily against the backrest. A newspaper rested on her lap.

Ted pressed against the wall just inside the door and announced himself with a timid "yeah, Ma." He feared a scolding for...he didn't know what.

"Stayin' out there kinda' late, ain't cha?'

Ted relaxed a little, but still expected punishment. "I was just out by the lake...was real nice out there, Ma." His active mind released its hold on the present and flashed an image of the sunset, the breeze, and the water.

"What if somethin' happened to you out there? We wouldn't find you 'til mornin'. By then, no tellin' what kinda' animal might be nibblin' on you."

Ted shuddered. "Yeah, Ma. I'll come home sooner next time." He wanted to block out the image of his mother's last remark, so he closed his eyes tightly. Summoning up courage, he repeated, as cheerfully as he could, "but it was real nice out there, Ma." His fancy once again took him to the lake and the wild horse that was beginning to trot around in his mind.

Ma Crockett made no reply and Ted listened for the sound of hoofbeats. His mind produced pictures of the fastest horse, dashing left and right among trees and leaping over bushes with such power that Ted's vivid imagination transported him to another place. His fingers clinched; his face brightened, reflecting the intoxication of the scene in his head. He became totally engrossed in what he saw, completely absorbed in the illusion that built in his mind like a balloon ready to burst. "Go, boy, go!" he shouted with such enthusiasm that his parents literally jumped in their chairs.

"Ted! What in the world ... what's the matter with you?" his mother questioned, leaning forward in her chair so far that it appeared she would tumble out of it. Her voice was demanding, disbelieving. Even Pa Crockett, jolted out of his contemplation, sat looking quizzically at Ted.

Ted straightened his back against the wall. "Ah...oh", he stammered, trying to compose himself. "Ah...sorry, Ma. I was just thinkin' 'bout somethin'... can I go to my room now?" He wanted desperately to be released from this embarrassment but dared not go without permission. He felt quite foolish as his mother and father stared at him for a moment before Ma Crockett dismissed him in a voice that reflected a degree of resignation.

"O.K. You can go." As Ted departed, a soft "G'night, Ma; G'night, Pa" echoed in the room.

Ted's parents watched him leave, but neither spoke. Then Ma Crockett leaned back in her chair and lowered her eyes, clasping her hands as though in prayer. Pa Crockett just flopped back and planted his elbows on the arms of the rocker. Each withdrew into private worlds until a grunt from Pa Crocket interrupted the reflections.

"See you in the mornin'," he rumbled as his big hulk wobbled out of the room.

"G'night," Ma Crockett replied and returned to her thoughts until drowsiness began nodding her head. Then she, too, surrendered, blew out the lantern and went to bed.

Saturday morning lit up with the sun sneaking up to the edge of the earth, peeking at a cloudless sky, and bursting upon the world with its light glaring. Ted awoke to the sun already well above the horizon and regretted waking up so late and missing part of the morning, but the previous evening, sleep had eluded him. He had tossed and turned as visions of the wild horse and plans for the morning return to the lake churned in his head.

Roland, his sixteen-year-old brother, was still asleep on his side of the double bed.

Ted got up and dressed quietly, enjoying the view out of the second story window. He and Roland shared the only upstairs room in the house, a room that had become their getaway. They enjoyed the privacy of their own nook. Now Ted crept down the stairs and skirted around the potbelly stove in the living room. Glancing into the kitchen, he went on past the closed door of his parents' room and glanced into the vacant room of his eighteen-year-old brother, Eugene. Everyone called him Gene. He was away in the war, somewhere in the Pacific–a place Ted had difficulty imagining.

He left the house through the mud-room and crossed the bare depression everyone called the front yard which, after heavy rains, became a lake of its own. But this morning, only dew from the cool night moistened everything, even the soil that stuck to the soles of his shoes. Blades of grass glistened with droplets of moisture and the tips of tree leaves held on to dewdrops that sparkled in the morning sun. As Ted thoughtlessly brushed against dew-laden branches of the mulberry tree at the edge of the yard, the cold wetness reminded him that he should have put on a jacket or sweater. But he continued past the chicken coop, now empty since the chickens had started their morning much earlier and were already scattered throughout the pasture, scratching and pecking at the damp earth.

At the woodpile, Ted stopped to enjoy the vista of the lake set in the clearing, and the pasture stretching all the way to the tree line. Scanning the area for signs of life, he observed only a few ducks spotting the lake and, near the bank, a rabbit nibbling at blades of wet grass.

Checking the area in the clearing where a fence met the water, his eyes explored the hidden spaces behind a grove of trees. But the only life there was blackbirds busily scurrying over the ground like a dark, moving carpet.

His hopes and expectations for the morning came to nothing and his disappointment was as heavy as the layer of wet soil that stuck to the soles of his shoes. He had expected the wild horse to be there. After all, he had dreamed it! He had visualized it! He had seen himself riding it! So now he expected the horse to be there.

His hopes shattered, Ted shuffled sadly to the pen where Spectrum came to the fence to greet him. Rubbing the horse's nose, Ted felt better. "You're a good horse, Spectrum. I can ride you. But I don't know nothin' 'bout the wild horse." Still, in his heart, the intense longing for his own horse saddened him. He felt alone and hugged Spectrum's head, squeezing so hard that the horse backed away. Ted reassured Spectrum and the two of them enjoyed each other like good friends.

"Breakfast's ready," Roland called from the porch.

After the meal, the boys swung into their chores. Actually, Ted moped into his.

Roland fed the pigs; Ted went to milk the cows. The milking gave Ted time to think about the wild horse, about the plan for the capture ...the capture! He hadn't thought seriously about it yet. A smile broke out on his face and his eyes widened as he drug out the realization. "Yeeeaaaah!" He stopped milking and thought for a moment, then drug the word out again. "Yeeeaaah!" In his mind, a picture formed that excited him and caused him to milk so vigorously that the cow kicked in protest, tipping the bucket and spilling some of the milk. "Aw, shucks!" Ted exclaimed, slamming his fist into the side of the cow. "Now look what you done!" Righting the bucket in time to save some of the milk, he scooted up to the utter and finished the chore. But the picture in his mind faded as he turned his attention to explanations he would need when he took the small amount of milk to the kitchen.

As noon approached, Ted was again on his way to the lake. He went straight to the far side where he had seen the horse the evening before. "Right about here," he muttered to himself as he studied the ground, now dried by the sun and wind, for tracks of the wild horse. He crossed and crisscrossed the area, finally discovering blurred imprints from which the dirt appeared to have been kicked back–the mark of running hooves. His heart responded to the discovery and, with it pounding in his chest, he followed the tracks to a path leading into the woods. The boys called this path 'Main Trail'.

Main Trail was the principle animal highway in the woods, a well-traveled path that snaked and twisted through the underbrush. Numerous passages of cattle and deer kept it open and free of growth. Like streets in a city, secondary trails crossed Main Trail and, about a half mile into the woods, Main Trail crossed a large clearing that, after a heavy rain, became a marshy bog. The boys called this clearing 'Big Swale'. It marked the limit of how far they were allowed to venture into the woods. Big Swale offered a place to stop, to consider and reflect, to turn around and go back, and it provided a stage for dramas to play out. Around Big Swale could be animals Ted had not discovered yet. It was about midway between the Crockett and the Brotchell homesteads, and it was best to stay clear of the Brotchells. It was safer, too, especially in the woods.

Now Ted followed the hoof prints into the woods and set out along Main Trail, alert to any sounds and movements. Underfoot, several kinds of footprints, most of which Ted recognized, showed that other animals had passed this way. Among these, distinct prints of horse hooves stared up at him. Several times, he stopped and listened in anxious, heart pounding anticipation, certain he heard a rustle in the brush. Each time, he was disappointed. "C'mon, horse. Come outta' there," he summoned, more to himself than to the horse. He was determined to check and investigate every sound and movement.

Arriving at the fringe of Big Swale, he paused. Big Swale in October was an expanse of dry stubble, the remains of the nibblings of cattle and deer–and horses! He emerged from the woods into the clearing under a cloud of disappointment, surprising a doe that made a hasty, tail-flicking retreat. Ted enjoyed watching the graceful, stretching way the deer ran, even through his gloominess, and he stopped to marvel.

The interlude boosted his spirits, but not much. Deciding to go back, he returned to Main Trail and arrived at the lake in brooding dissatisfaction. Ignoring the crawfish that slid into its water-filled hole as he approached the bank, he sat down in his favorite well-worn spot and looked deep into the water. Whenever he felt moody, he would sit like this for a long time, hardly moving. This was one of those times.

The rest of the day melted into a week that passed slowly. Ted found it difficult to concentrate on school work, especially on Thursday when one of his classmates came to school on a horse.

"Can I ride 'em?" he asked.

"Naw!" answered his classmate.

"Why?"

"Dunno '. My Pa just told me not to let anyone ride' em."

But I can pet 'em, cain't I?"

"Guess that's O.K."

Ted spent recess and lunchtime admiring and petting the horse. He dreamed some, too, for the horse looked like the one at the lake, black with a flowing mane and long tail. Ted even wondered if this actually could be the wild horse he had seen. His mind whirled with visions of what might be. After school, as he watched his classmate ride off, he imagined himself on his own horse - the sleekest, fastest, proudest horse around. He would depart the schoolyard to the envy of all his classmates.

On Saturday morning, Ted woke early but stayed in bed, thinking about his twelfth birthday. Today! Twelve years old! Even though birthdays were hardly celebrated in the Crockett home, Ted felt special. He thought about twelve as a dozen; twelve was on the threshold of the teen years; twelve was a mark of growing up, a departure from childhood. At least he hoped everyone would see it that way. In some way, he would make it a special day for himself. Maybe his mother would bake him a cake. If not, that would be O.K. Disappointing, but O.K. He decided to do something special just for himself–maybe catch a horse!

As he lay there, thoughts of birthday delights floated around in his thoughts until a dark horse, its coat shiny and smooth, trotted onto the scene in his head. Ted saw himself grab a handful of mane and flip himself onto its back. He saw himself kick the horse into a long, stretching, leg-reaching run so swift that he had to hold like a tick to the horse's flying mane and clamp his legs around its belly for a hold. He was now totally engrossed in the events playing in his imagination, the wind rushing over his face, streaming back his hair like the flying tail of the horse.

"Hey!" Roland shouted at him from the real world. The exc1amation jerked Ted back into real life.

Roland was propped up on one elbow. "You havin' some kinda' nightmare or somethin' ?"

Ted flushed. "Guess I was dreamin'."

"Musta' been...shoulda' seen yourself," Roland mumbled, grinning as he flopped back onto his pillow.

"What'd I do?"

Roland just smiled. "Shoulda' seen yourself."

Ted was now fully awake and wanted to talk. "Rolan'!" he began, then paused. He just knew that his brother wouldn't believe his story about the horse.

"What?"

Now Ted felt cornered, but he didn't have the courage to talk about the horse.

"Today's my birthday!" he suddenly blurted out.

"Don't matter none," Roland said as his head came up off the pillow. "You're still not old...you're still my *little* brother." Roland grinned as he slammed his pillow over Ted's head and started giving him the traditional whacks across the butt.

The boys jostled and wrestled and Ted kicked and laughed so vigorously that he fell out of bed before Roland even got to number nine. With Ted on the floor and Roland looking down on him from the edge of the bed, the two laughed and giggled like boys much younger than sixteen and twelve.

"What's that ruckus up there?" Ma Crockett yelled from downstairs.

"Sorry we woke you," Roland called down. "Didn't mean to." He quickly searched for something else to say. "We're celebratin' Ted's birthday."

"Kinda' early for that," Ma Crockett yawned as she shuffled off toward the kitchen.

About mid-morning, Pa Crockett called to Ted. "You better come with me to the barn." His voice was harsh; his face, stern.

Ted stiffened at the command. All kinds of misdeeds that he might have done flashed through his mind. Normally, when his Pa asked him to go to the barn with him, it meant punishment of some kind. Sometimes, like now, he feared his father. He wanted to ask him why he chose today, his birthday, to punish him for...for what? Didn't his father know it was his birthday? He trembled a little on the way to the barn.

"Come in here," Pa Crockett commanded, opening the barn door and removing a horse halter off a nail. But by the time he turned to face Ted, he couldn't hold back the teasing grin and he playfully draped the halter over Ted's head.

Ted was confused, stunned, but after a moment, he caught on to his father's playfulness and the worry faded from his face.

Pa Crockett smiled broadly. "The horse you call Spectrum—he's yours now. You know how to take care of 'em and I know you can look after 'em," he said as he gave a little pull on the halter. "I might still need 'em sometime, but not much."

Ted and his father hugged each other and laughed so hard that Ted fell backward onto the hay. Getting up, he grinned and giggled at this father who whacked him affectionately. It was a great moment, a wonderful moment. Ted had never seen his father be more gentle and affectionate, and he treasured the moment.

With the halter still around his neck, Ted puffed up his chest–not much of a puff up, given his slender frame–and in long, stiff strides, strolled out of the barn like a seasoned cowboy, although an unseasoned wetness glistened in his eyes. Stretching himself to his tallest, he strolled into the pen and approached Spectrum in such uncommonly long strides that he almost lost his balance. After greeting Spectrum in an unusual display of nose rubbing and neck hugging, he slipped the halter over the horse's head, grabbed a handful of mane and flipped his lanky body onto the horse's back.

He adjusted himself to sit so straight and tall that Pa Crockett chuckled to Roland, who had come to the gate:

"He looks like a board standing on end on the horse's back."

Roland chuckled back, "yeah, like a one-by-four."

Pa Crocket opened the gate and Ted, taking the cue, nudged Spectrum forward with a slight squeeze of his knees. Spectrum, having grown accustomed to the light body on his back, responded and took up his normal, slow walk. Passing his father and brother at the gate, Ted beamed at them a grin so broad that it appeared to separate his chin from the rest of his face.

"Still looks like a board," Pa Crockett chuckled as he closed the gate.

Ted did not hear, for he had just given Spectrum another squeeze of his knees and Spectrum responded with his top speed: a slow trot that caused Ted to bounce like...well, like a board. But Ted felt good in the new ownership, turning the horse this way and that just for the fun of it. Then he set out in the direction of the lake. The duo had made many trips to the lake together but this one was different. Spectrum was now *his* horse. Once again, Ted swelled his chest, straightened his back and squared his shoulders with pride.

At the lake, Ted remained glued to Spectrum's back as he rode over the open pasture.

At one point, he took out his harmonica and played hard, drawing and puffing on it as though he wanted to blow it apart. The song was especially tense and emotional and Ted ended it with long, drawn-out, wavering notes that faded away until his lungs no longer gave him any more breath. Leaning forward, he hugged Spectrum's neck, burying his face in the mane.

"Hey, Ted!" The call seemed to come from far away. Ted returned slowly from his reverie to the present and looked toward the house where Roland was waving and approaching from the woodpile. "Time for dinner. You're gonna' grow to the horse's back if you don't get down once in a while."

Ted waved back, not realizing that the time had slipped by so quickly. Pointing Spectrum toward the barn, he gave the horse a soft kick and enjoyed Spectrum's tired trot all the way back to the pen, still bouncing on his back like a board.

"You walk funny," Roland joked as he joined up with Ted on the way to the house.

Ted only smiled. "He's mine, Rolan'! He's just mine!

"Yeah."

The next morning, Sunday, Ted sat impatiently in the church pew, his body captive to the worship. But his mind wandered. Even Wanda, sitting across the isle, failed to bring his mind totally into the church with her flirty smile. On past Sundays, her smile caused a tingle in his body and he always smiled back. Certainly Ma Crockett would have slapped the tingle out of him had she known of this behavior in church. She had already warned him twice about showings of fondness toward her and he concluded that it must be sinful to be friendly with Wanda. He tried not to think how hard it is to be perfect.

Back home after the church service, Ted nosed around the kitchen. "When we gonna' eat, Ma?'

His mother didn't even look away from the pot of chicken soup boiling on the kerosene stove. "Patience, Ted. What's your hurry?"

Ted didn't answer and went into the living room where Pa Crockett and Roland were rumpling newspapers in front of their faces.

He sat down to do the same but it wasn't long before the call, "dinner's ready," came from the kitchen.

At the table, Ted slurped soup and eagerly ate the boiled chicken meat that had been fished out of it. Grabbing two pieces of pastry, he announced to his mother, as he always did when he wanted to leave: "I'm not hungry no more."

At his mother's customary response of "go ahead, then," Ted scooted away from the table and hurried toward the door.

"That boy's gonna' turn inside out over that horse," Ma Crockett commented as she watched Ted shoot through the door. "He's been ridin' 'em for a long time ... what's his hurry today?" Sometimes, Ma Crockett felt like she was not privy to everything going on around the homestead.

"Ma," Roland offered, "it's Ted's horse now. Yesterday, Pa gave it to him…for his birthday."

"Lord, save us!" she exclaimed as she started to clear the table, "That's all he needs."

She clanked a few pans. "Now it'll be like pullin' hen's teeth to get 'em to do anything 'round here."

Ma Crockett's disapproval simply floated out the window on the breeze that flowed through the house, for Pa Crockett seldom asked for advice nor paid much attention to criticism. He was, at that very moment, aiming his hulk toward the bedroom to indulge in a Sunday after dinner nap.

About mid-afternoon, friends of the family arrived for a visit. There was Ma and Pa Berenek, Christopher–everyone called him Chris–age fifteen, and Wanda, age twelve. After loud greetings and much laughter, the parents went into the house to sit and talk. Eventually, they might move to the porch, still talking. Chris and Roland disappeared to explore the woods, pasture and field. Normally, Ted went with them. Today, however, he wanted to show off his horse to Wanda.

"Come see what I got for my birthday," he beckoned to her.

Ma Crockett gave Ted a disapproving look. Ted pretended not to notice.

"Come look! You'll never guess." He led Wanda to the gate of the pen, and pointed.

"Spectrum!" he said with pride.

"You got this horse for your birthday?"

"Yeah! Pa gave 'em to me yesterday…scared the wits outta' me first. I thought he was gonna' paddle me for somethin' when he took me to the barn. But then he gave me Spectrum."

"Wow, your own horse! Why'd you name him Spectrum, anyway?"

Ted puffed up with pride. "Long ago, when I first started to ride 'em, I saw a rainbow in his eye an' I remembered from school that the colors of the rainbow are called a spectrum. "

"That's cute."

"Well, I never heard of anyone else havin' a horse by that name, an' I like bein' different. Wanna' ride 'em?"

"Well, you know I don't ride much…an' I'm wearin' this dress," she said modestly. "Maybe I better not today." Noticing Ted's disappointment, she added, "next time we come, I'll wear somethin' different so I can ride."

"He's real easy to ride. Watch!" Before Wanda could say, "I believe you," Ted was over the gate and on Spectrum's back, pacing him around the pen. Then he guided him to the gate, nudging Spectrum forward so his head extended over the gate to Wanda. He dismounted.

"You like 'em?" he asked as Wanda politely petted Spectrum's nose.

"Ted, I've seen this horse lotsa' times…an' I've seen you ride 'em lotsa' times."

"Yeah, but that was before he was mine. Now he's mine."

"Still the same horse."

"No he ain't," Ted protested. "Now he's mine. It's not the same."

"Well, he's real nice." After a pause, Wanda stammered, "an'...uh...happy birthday, though it's a day late." She squinted at him seriously. "I didn't bring you anything…in fact, I even forgot it was your birthday."

"That's O. K. I really had a good day," Ted assured her as he shifted his attention to rubbing Spectrum's nose. "Ain't he somethin'?" Petting Spectrum's neck, he circled his arm under it to give the horse a hug and unexpectedly touched Wanda's hand on the other side. A tingle rushed through his body as he felt her squeeze back, ever so briefly. But this made him feel uncomfortable and he jerked his hand back, alarming Spectrum. The horse backed away like an opening curtain, leaving Ted and Wanda facing each other. She grinned at him and he quivered back an uncertain smile. The moment held very briefly before they both turned and silently pretended to show interest in Spectrum.

Standing against the gate, neither spoke. Wanda held her smiling gaze on Spectrum.

But Ted wrestled within himself, putting the enjoyment of finally owning Spectrum against the rising, uncertain warmth from Wanda that made him feel weak. The two emotions would give him enough conflict to last the whole week.

2

Tragedy

Big Swale was like a sanctuary locked from the outside world by encircling woods, a little universe of privacy. But sometimes it was a stage, supporting spectacular performances. This late afternoon in October, Big Swale became a stage. Two white tail buck deer made their stand at the western edge, squaring off at about ten feet. They challenged each other with lowered heads and quivering neck and leg muscles. Slowly, like a wound up spring in the first stage of unwinding, they rotated and moved toward each other. Suddenly, responding to some silent signal, they charged with such a resounding head-on crash that the tip of an antler shot away like a bullet. Now they struggled, pushing and shoving and pulling in great fury, their hooves digging into the dry soil and stirring up a cloud of dust. The mighty combat grew into vigorous assaults of push, pull, turn, jerk, and twist.

Near center stage, a doe casually observed the contest with neutral interest while continuing to munch dry grass. Appearing unconcerned, she returned to nibbling the stubble at her feet.

As quickly as the charge had exploded, it stopped, a swirling dust cloud shrouding the bucks with their antlers still engaged. Then again, as though on signal, they pulled, jerked, twisted and shoved only to stop once more, antlers still engaged. Now the fight exploded again and the bucks, in the swirling dust, with their antlers now inseparable, enjoined a mighty battle to break free. Abruptly, they stopped and stood as one long shadow in the dust cloud.

Blam! Blam! Without warning, gunshots blasted into the clearing and echoed across Big Swale. The doe bolted and in long, tail-flashing leaps, she vanished into the woods. At the same time, one of the bucks collapsed, almost causing the other to lose its balance. The buck standing pulled and jerked vigorously, trying to break free of his dead opponent. He dragged the dead one about until they both disappeared into the brush. Blam! Another gunshot shattered the afternoon and Ted heard a jubilant shout: "Got 'em!" Other voices joined in with victorious exclamations that could be heard over the entire stage of Big Swale.

Ted had had a front row seat to the drama that played out in front of him. He had seen it all up to the time the bucks disappeared into the woods. It so happened that he had been riding Spectrum along Main Trail, approaching the eastern fringe of Big Swale when he had glimpsed the deer and had dismounted only moments before the bucks crashed together. He had stood wide-eyed and breathless, marveling at the encounter, when the first two shots rang out. Now he could hear the excited jabbering of the unseen hunters, and they sounded like the Brotchells, the mean and uncaring ragtag from the neighboring homestead.

Instantly, Ted hated them, even more than he normally did. Anger twisted his face and urged him to run at them and...do what? Common sense, flavored with sobering fear, made him reluctant to confront them, and he restrained his compulsion.

Disappointed, frustrated and mad, he turned Spectrum around and led him back down the trail, trying to be quiet but almost not caring if he made any noise. After going a distance, Ted felt safe enough to flip himself onto Spectrum's back. His legs quivered with the urge to kick Spectrum into a gallop, allowing the horse instead to take up his own pace. Riding along Main Trail, Ted reviewed the scene he had just witnessed. His anger melted into wonder at the striking fierceness of white tail bucks in battle. This was not the first time he had seen such an event but it left him, as always, awestruck. He wondered about what the outcome would have been had the Brotchells not interfered. He could only wonder and speculate.

That night, Ted lay in his bed unable to fall asleep. His mind kept playing and re-playing the Big Swale scene of tragedy and horror. Roland was downstairs helping his mother nurse his father's wound. Disbelief and anger kept Ted awake. He wrestled with anger at the Brotchells as he reviewed the events at Big Swale. He struggled to reconcile the circumstances when the Brotchells shot the deer, sending a bullet into the upper part of his father's left shoulder. Unknown to Ted, his father had not been too far from where Ted had stood watching the deer. He reasoned that his father must have followed the deer and was stalking them for a shot of his own, but the Brotchells beat him to it. So close, Ted thought. He and his father each had been unbelievably close, yet oblivious of each other.

Ted tried to sequence the events that brought his father to Big Swale. His father probably spotted a buck and a doe in the clearing beyond the lake and had hurried into the house to secure a gun and stomp out without saying a word. He always did that when pursuing pest or game, and the activity always created unbearable suspense for Ted. Now Ted imagined the chase: his father cautiously following the deer–Pa Crockett knew much about the behavior of wild creatures–stalking silently. In his mind, Ted saw his father arriving at Big Swale just moments before he himself had. They had both been quiet, neither knowing of the other's presence. Ted could not believe the coincidence as he imagined his father watching the bucks confronting each other, just as he had. Then, when the shots came, he pictured the gun falling from Pa Crockett's hand as his body followed it to the ground. Ted just could not believe it all.

Now lying in bed, thinking and wondering, he felt his chest tighten with hatred for the Brotchells. He reviewed his father's description of how, after he was shot, he had lain on the ground, bleeding, knowing by the voices that the hunters were the Brotchell boys. "I almost shouted for help," he had said, "but decided to lie there and die rather than have them Brotchells find me." Wincing as he took a breath, he had concluded, "I figgered anythin ' was better than facin' 'em."

Ted knew that his father didn't mean that he really would rather die, but he understood the bitterness the families held for each other. As he thought deeply about this, Roland entered the room and startled him.

"How's Pa, Rolan', how's he?" Anxiety colored Ted's query.

"He's kinda' weak. Lost some blood. Cain't do nothin' with his left hand."

Ted's heart went downstairs as he pondered his father's fate. A restless uneasiness overcame him and he wondered about the extent of his father's pain and if his father could sleep. The bed jostled as Roland settled in for the night. Suddenly, Ted realized that he was still holding a fearsome secret, having been reluctant to reveal it.

"Rolan'!" he said in a low voice.

"Huh?" punctuated the silence.

"Rolan' ... "

"Whatcha want?"

"Rolan', I seen them bucks fightin' today."

Roland sprang off his pillow and bounced onto an elbow. "You did?"

His brother's voice frightened Ted and dampened his desire to say anything more. But he continued bravely. "Yeah! I came upon 'em just when they crashed head-on. They was really fightin', Rolan'! You shoulda' seen 'em!"

"I wouldn't care to see 'ern if it meant Pa getting' shot." Roland paused and looked at Ted. "How come you didn't run into Pa?'

Ted began feeling bad about even bringing it up. "I came home right after the last shot. I got scared when I heard them Brotchells talkin'. Got mad, too…but I didn't see Pa anywhere. He musta' been real quiet." Feeling helpless, Ted released a lungful of air, making a whooshing sound. "Wish I'd known he was there." After a pause, he continued. "Just think, Rolan'. Pa was right there...not too far from me, shot...an' I never knew it." Ted's chin quivered, an event that usually preceded tears.

"How come you didn't say nothin' about this before?"

"I was scared to…and there was no time, with getting Pa into the house and to bed an' everythin'… ."

Both boys flopped back onto the bed. Silence crept out of the night and settled into the room as Ted stared open-eyed into the darkness. Roland tugged at the covers and rolled onto his side. "But he got home O.K. That's the main thing," he said as he sank his head into the pillow.

"Yeah! It's a wonder he did…look who brung 'em." Ted paused to work up more hate.

"I never thought them Brotchells would go to that much trouble for anybody. Bet they woulda' just as soon left Pa there, hurtin' or not."

Roland made no remark and once again silence settled into the room as a breeze drifted in through a half-open window, crept over the boys and, through a window on the other side of the room, escaped into the night. There, the moon, set in a star-lit sky, smiled its first quarter. The bed jostled as Roland stirred again. Soon, he drew long, heavy breaths. But Ted couldn't sleep. He slipped out of bed, stole out of the room and made his way down the stairs.

In the kitchen, the flame of a stubby candle created an irregular dance of lights and shadows. Candlelight also flickered in his parent's room. Peeping in, he saw his mother applying a new bandage to his father's shoulder. Ted took a few moments to observe the large form of his father, a strong man whom only a major catastrophe like this could confine to bed. Ted felt a lump in his throat as he slowly entered the room.

"You should be asleep by now," his mother advised. "I couldn't sleep, Ma. Just kept thinkin' about Pa."

The eyelids on his father's hawk-like, closely set eyes opened slightly and he peered at Ted. Somewhat timidly, Ted approached the bed. He was scarcely able to force more than a whisper.

"How ya feelin', Pa?' His father appeared weak, and the sight moistened Ted's eyes and turned on that switch near the heart that softens the muscles, quivers the chin and sometimes causes the breath to inhale in spasms.

"I'll be O.K." His father labored on the words. "It hurts now and I'm a little weak..." He took a deep breath and winced. "I'll get strong again."

Ma Crockett walked out of the room, balancing a pan of crimson water. Ted knelt down, took two knee steps and pressed against the bed, next to his father.

"Pa," he whispered, "when you get O.K. and strong again, I have somethin' to tell you...it's real important." Ted fought to still the quiver of his chin and the waver in his voice. "So hurry an' get O.K."

His father's head turned to face his son. "Cain't you tell me now?"

Ted looked at his father, a sight that precipitated a small stream of tears down his cheeks. "I wanna' wait til you're O.K."

"Be waitin' to hear it," his father muttered as he turned his head back and closed his eyes.

"Late now…better go…to bed."

Ted tried to shut off his sniffling. Inhaling deeply, he stuttered a "G'night, Pa" and left the room. Meeting his mother as she came out of the kitchen, he threw her a shaky "G'night, Ma" and proceeded up the stairs to his room. Lying in bed again, he pictured his father; he pictured the bucks fighting; he pictured the Brotchells. The dark face of revenge began rearing its head. "You just wait," he threatened through clinched teeth and tight lips, not even worrying about waking Roland. "Just wait! I'll get you guys," he hissed. Then he buried his head deep into the pillow and again saw his father, the bucks fighting, the Brotchells, the deer fighting, his father, the Brotchells, his father, the bucks, his father…

3

Ted's Folly

Ted woke with a start, the morning sun much too bright for his wakening eyes. He had spent a restless night. His dreams, more like nightmares, featured Spectrum, his father, the mysterious wild horse and the Brotchells. But it was his father's tragedy that stood out in his mind as he lay in bed, re-living the scene that took place in Big Swale the day before. He felt a tightening in his stomach, even though he had just awakened, and his hands clinched into fists. He became determined somehow to stand up and avenge his father's injury and decided to confront the Brotchells and inflict on them some horrible blow equal to the harm they inflicted on his father. Getting out of bed, he slipped into his clothes, rather clumsily.

"Gosh, Ted, cain't you be a little more quiet?" Roland protested as he rolled over in bed.

Ted did not respond, but hurried downstairs and slammed himself down in a chair at the breakfast table, opposite Ma Crocket.

"Had a bad night, huh?"

"Yeah!" He relaxed enough to wolf down some breakfast. "How's Pa?"

"He's still asleep. I'm really worried about 'em".

Ted did not respond but got up and hurried out the door, stomped across the yard and made his way to the pen where Spectrum had his nose in the feed trough. As Ted approached, Spectrum raised his head and looked at him, and Ted walked over and hugged his neck. "We'll get 'em, boy," he promised. "You an' me

... we'll get 'em." He ran his hand over the horse's neck. "You finish eatin', then we'll get 'em."

Ted ached from the tightness of the anger in him as he sat down to watch Spectrum eat. He liked his horse. No, he loved his horse, although at this moment love seemed out of place. Spectrum stepped over to the water trough and Ted saw it was time to go. Boosted by feelings of revenge, he led Spectrum out of the pen, flipped onto his back and turned him in the direction of the morning's destiny.

Spectrum walked leisurely and Ted did not urge him on. Rather, he turned his thoughts to what he would do when he reached his destination. He really had no idea what he could do since the Brotchells were such a mean bunch and they would just as soon stomp on him as look at him. At least that's the way he felt. The rhythm and sway of Spectrum's walk had a hypnotizing effect on Ted and he let Spectrum follow Main Trail to Big Swale and beyond. All too soon, as though carried through time, he found himself in forbidden land, nearing the Brotchell homestead.

At some distance, he brought Spectrum to a stop and trained his eyes toward their house and the corral. Spectrum stood obediently while Ted wrestled with the fear that suddenly gripped him. He began to doubt himself: "What am I doin' here, anyway?" Right away, he answered himself: "To avenge my father." Somewhat encouraged by his own reply, he searched his mind for a plan but strong misgivings about his daring began to surface. He shifted nervously on Spectrum's back and fortified himself with the thought of his purpose for being there. Thoughts of his father were his strength and the Brotchell shooting was the fire in his belly. Anger began to replace fear and to encourage him. He slid off his horse, still not knowing what he was going to do.

Tying Spectrum to a tree, he began to stalk the Brotchell homestead until he came to the edge of the woods where the thinning brush faded into a clearing that surrounded the house. Squatting behind a bush, Ted felt a fear that was more like terror. Sweat formed on his face and he wrestled with the wisdom of going on, pitting revenge against fear. For the moment, revenge was winning. Still with no plan, he decided to go on, relying on cunning to spot an opportunity to…he didn't know what.

As he looked over the homestead, the corral and the horses in it caught his attention.

Without even making the decision, he began sneaking in that direction, circling around through the woods so the corral would be between him and the house. There, calling on all his courage, he sprinted to the corral in a low crouch.

The five horses in the corral raised their heads to acknowledge his arrival as he knelt down beside the wooden rail fence. He breathed heavily as his heart pounded in his chest. "What next?" he asked himself. A vengeful thought suggested that he open the gate and lead the horses away. He thought some more. Maybe he should sneak over to the smokehouse and… .

Suddenly, his scheming was interrupted by a sound coming from the house. Peering through the corral, between the rails and the legs of the horses, Ted saw one of the Brotchell men come out of the house, stand on the porch and look over the area, especially gazing at the corral. Instantly, Ted felt terrible fear–no, horrible terror–no, heart-stopping panic. Cowering by the corral fence, he questioned his foolishness again, challenging his wisdom about what he was doing. For the moment, all he could do was remain still. If he could just calm down his pounding heart.

The Brotchell enjoyed a stretch and a yawn, then started walking toward the corral. A tall man, he walked with a determined stride, all the time looking around as though expecting to find some pest intruding into his domain. But it appeared to Ted that he himself was not yet discovered.

Ted was so scared that he could not think. Looking at the small hay barn next to the corral, he considered trying to hide behind it. Maybe he could slither over there like a snake. Instead, with the Brotchell half the way to the corral, a terrified Ted jumped up and dashed toward the woods like a rabbit flushed out by hounds. A startled horse whinnied. The Brotchell spotted Ted, yelled and gave chase. The rest of the Brotchell family inside the house, hearing the commotion, poured out onto the porch but, by the time they realized what was happening, the pursuer was just moments away from having Ted in his grip.

Ted was absolutely terrified. Running for his life–he felt certain that he was–he heard the pounding of Brotchell feet behind him before he felt big hands grasp his shoulders. His legs gave way, more from the expectation of what might happen than from the hands grabbing him, and he rolled forward in a small cloud of dust. When he stopped rolling, he lay looking up at the towering form of the Brotchell. From this position, he looked like a giant, and about as strong. Ted lay on the ground shaking in terror as the other Brotchell men came running.

"Well, looky here," one of them said.

"You look like a scairt rabbit," another observed. And that's about how Ted felt.

"What you doin' here?" a third wanted to know.

Ted opened his mouth, but was speechless. He cringed at the thought of what might come.

"Let's take 'em to the house and let Pa have a look." The pronouncement sounded like a declaration of victory, like one pronounced after the capture of a possum caught raiding the chicken coop. Surely the Brotchell men knew who he was, for they had been neighbors–although not good ones–for many years. Still, they half dragged Ted to the house.

At the porch, Ted looked up to see Ma and Pa Brotchell standing and looking down at him. A girl–slim, straight and tall–stood behind her parents with her back against the house. Her long face, framed by straight hair falling to her shoulders, was plain, expressionless. She seemed not to belong to this household. Pa Brotchell, hovering like a vulture, seemed to embody all the cruelty in the world. His eyes, set wide on each side of a small nose, peered out between slits of squinted eyelids. His lips bared teeth as in a grin, giving his whole face a scowl like that of a growling dog. Ma Brotchell didn't appear much kinder. Her heavy eyebrows and upside down mouth showed sternness, a 'do as I say' attitude and she appeared capable of enforcing her commands.

Rarely had Ted seen the Brotchells this close, but they had always scared him, even at a distance. Now, they terrified him.

Behind him, a horse whinnied and a voice announced "look what I found." Ted looked around to see Spectrum being led toward the gathering by one of the men. Now he really was scared.

"You're a Crockett, ain't cha?" Pa Brotchell barked in a gruff voice, although he surely knew the answer. "Whatcha' want here?" he demanded. Standing on the porch, looking menacingly down at Ted, he looked like a judge–and executioner–presiding over Ted's life.

Ted's legs felt weak and his throat felt so dry he couldn't talk.

"Well?" tundered Pa Brotchell.

"Let 'em go," Ma Brotchell pleaded. "Look at 'em—Scarder than a rabbit with a cayote on 'is tail. Just a boy. Don't see where he can do us no harm." She spoke in a matter-of-fact voice, without expression or emotion. "Let 'em go," she repeated as she turned and disappeared into the house. The girl–tall, straight and expressionless–followed her.

The short silence that followed was broken by Pa Brotchell's decree: "Keep 'is horse an' let 'em go. Maybe that'll teach 'em not to come sneakin' 'round here."

Ted felt like he had been sentenced in court.

"Git outa' here!" one of the men shouted. Another, the one who had found Spectrum, swung himself up onto Spectrum's back as a terrified Ted backed away from the house and turned to run toward the woods. The Brotchell on Spectrum began to follow.

Glancing back, Ted felt frustration and anger mix with the fear inside him. "Spectrum in the hands of the Brotchells," he muttered. At the edge of the clearing, he looked back at Spectrum with the Brotchell on his back. He saw the others at the house, standing and watching. The sight angered his so much that it felt like a fire burning away all fear and doubt. The rage in him snapped all good sense and, calling on all his strength and courage, he ran toward his horse.

"Spectrum!" he shouted. "Throw 'em, Spectrum," he commanded as though his horse were a trained animal. "Buck, Spectrum! Up, Spectrum!" he yelled as he ran. "Throw 'em!" As Ted neared the horse, the Brotchell turned Spectrum and kicked Ted in the chest. He fell backward, but got up on the strength of hate and, waiting just a moment, he lunged for his horse again, shouting: "Spectrum! Throw 'em, Spectrum!" The Brotchell kicked him again and Ted, feeling a boot in his stomach, fell back to the ground again.

"Git outa' here, ya' runt," snarled the Brotchell. Git goin'!" he commanded in words dripping with scorn.

Ted tried to get up, but the pain in his chest and stomach sapped all his strength and he dropped back to the ground. Bravely, he looked up. The Brotchell sat astride Spectrum like a conquering general. "Git!" he barked at Ted as though he was chasing a pest away from the hen house.

With great effort, Ted got to his feet and, hunched over in pain, stumbled into the woods, going just far enough to be out of sight of the Brotchell house. Looking back to make sure that he was not being followed any more, he collapsed by a tree. Hurting and aching, he lay there in misery, listening to the whinny and snort of horses. He suspected that Spectrum was being led into the Brotchell corral, and that made his pain worse.

As he listened, the thought of his horse in the Brotchell corral became more unbearable than the pain in his body. Frustration, anger and hatred began to overcome his physical misery as he tried to think of what he could do to get his horse back. Surely, he could not return home without his horse. His father would certainly punish him for losing Spectrum through this kind of foolishness. The sudden memory of his father hit him like the Brotchell's boot. Thoughts flashed by quickly–his father, shot by the Brotchells, lying in the woods. Shot! The Brotchells didn't care.

In just moments, the picture in his mind increased and fortified his frustration and anger. Determined to get his horse back, and scarcely aware of his action, he got to his feet and began moving in the direction of the corral, stumbling to the edge of the woods in time to see the Brotchell men walking from the corral toward the house, doubling over with arm-flailing laughter. Although he could not understand the words, he felt certain they were laughing at him. "I'll show you, ya' scum!" Ted hissed through tightly twisted lips.

After everyone had entered the house, his attention shifted to the corral. Spectrum!

There he was, in there with the Brotchell horses like a common animal. Ted even hated their horses, and the sight was too much for him. His fists tightened and his jaws clinched so tightly that his bottom lip pouted. Glancing toward the house, he dashed, as best as he could, across the clearing to the corral. He slipped between the rails ofthe fence and continued toward Spectrum. The horses, already restless, began to whinny and mill around. In the midst, Ted pushed and groped and pounded his fist into the side of any horse that got in his way.

The action created panic among the horses. One of them brushed Ted, knocking him to the ground. A moment later, a sharp pain exploded in his leg and shot through his body; then another. He squirmed and tried to get to his feet. This new pain, added to the old, became unbearably excruciating. He almost didn't care as he lay curled up on the ground with hooves stepped all around him.

"Whoa, there, whoa!"

The commands seemed like they came from miles away, but Ted became aware of Brotchells mingling with the horses. Horses and Brotchells, swirling and mixing! While the Brotchells tried to calm the milling animals, Ted tried to get to his feet but managed only to get to a sitting position. He heard a sharp crack, like a fence rail breaking, but he paid no attention to it. Sitting hunched over on the ground in the midst of restless horses and unpredictable Brotchells, he felt pain stabbing his body like fingers of lightening.

As the horses calmed down, he could feel–he didn't even have to look–he could feel the presence of a Brotchell looking down at him. Contempt oozed out of the Brotchell's mouth. "Well, you squirt!" he hissed. Disdain dripped from his voice like water from a twisted rag. "You just couldn't leave it alone, could ya? You squirt!"

Total and complete helplessness intensified Ted's pain. Curling up on the ground again, he surrendered all resistance and began to cry—a cry of pain and frustration, of hate and helplessness; a sobbing, shaking cry of despair. He felt totally overcome and conquered.

"Look at 'em. Didn't have enough sense t'go home." The voice of the Brotchell was hollow and empty of feeling. Ted could feel the lack of even a little pity or sympathy.

"Hey, squirt, quit your whimperin'." The words were as sharp as the horse's hooves. Pa Brotchell intervened. "Looks like he's hurt. You boys better load 'em up an' take 'em home. I don't think he'll try this again." He spoke with no more feeling than if he was giving his sons orders to go get a load of hay.

With some protests and grumbling, one of them backed a pickup to the corral. They prodded Ted as he staggered and stumbled and finally crawled into the bed of the pickup. There, he collapsed - battered, hurt and broken.

"I don't wanna' take 'em. You take 'em," one of the men said as he slammed the tailgate shut.

"Not me!" protested another.

"I'm not gonna' neither," objected a third.

Pa Brotchell adjudicated. "All three of you pile in there an' take 'em. Now git goin'." Lying curled up on the rusted bed of the pickup, Ted was not interested in the squabble. The coldness of the argument just angered him more but he felt too battered to do anything. He heard some more grumbling, then felt the vehicle shudder as doors were opened and the men got into the cab. He winced as the pickup jerked forward and bounced toward the Crockett homestead. Each rut in the road felt like a chasm; every bump felt like a mountain. Somewhere along the way, Ted surrendered to the mercy of unconsciousness.

4

Harsh Consequences

Ted lay in bed, staring at the ceiling. Some parts of his body screamed with pain, too sore and tender even to touch, a result of the beating from the Brotchells and the trampling by the horses the day before. Through clouded thinking, he considered his fortune and his agony: he had no broken bones but, oh how his body hurt!

Lying in a puddle of self-pity, he doubted he could ever avenge his father, or ever catch the wild horse. In the sour hatred he felt for the Brotchells, his tormented mind kept replaying the tragedies of the day before. Recreating the corral scene, he determined that he would have succeeded had he just controlled himself and kept a cool head; if he had not ruined his plan, even though he really had no plan. After all, he thought, he knew his way around horses and being knocked down and kicked was just a fluke. Anyway, the embarrassment of it made the physical pain even worse.

"Here, Ted, eat some of this." His mother startled him as she entered the room. "You hurt pretty bad, huh?"

"Yeah, Ma. Everythin' hurts 'cept my tongue."

Ma Crockett smiled at this report as she began covering black and blue places on Ted's body with wet, cool towels.

"That feels better, Ma." Ted thought his mother had the patience of a saint, for not only did she have his father to care for, but now she also had to take care of him. The thought made him uncomfortable and he felt a real ache in his heart for causing her this extra worry and care. "Ma, I'm sorry for… ."

"Hey, Ted, how ya' feelin'?" Roland interrupted as he bounded into the room and sat on the edge of the bed. He studied his brother closely. "Darn, you look like somethin' swallowed you an' spit you back out," he tried to joke.

"Yeah," Ted moaned. "That's about the way I feel. I hate them Brotchells." Ted tightened his face. "Why do they have to be like that—so mean?" A bit of self-pity formed a tear in his eye. "Did they bring Spectrum back, Rolan…did they?" There was a painful hope in his voice. When Roland did not answer, he asked again. "Did they?" The pit of his stomach tightened and he began to feel sick.

Roland's cheerfulness melted like an ice cube in hot water. "They brought 'em back."

His voice was matter-of-fact and his mouth felt dry.

"I don't un'erstan' them Brotchells, Ted reflected. He lay still and spoke softly. "They beat me up, keep Spectrum, and then when I…" his voice trailed off in a blush…"when I go back to get 'em, they bring me an' Spectrum home. I don't un'erstan' it, Rolan'."

Roland forced his words. "They probably did that 'cause they saw how hurt you was, an' they sure didn't wanna' take care of you." There was a silent pause. "A'n cause… " Looking into Ted's tortured and expectant face, Roland continued but the tremble in his voice reflected the sorry he felt for his brother. "Cause Spectrum's leg got broke in the corral." Ted cringed. The milling of the horses flashed through his mind as Roland continued. "At least that's what the Brotchells said. They brought 'em in the truck after they brought you."

Ted cringed again. Deep in his memory he heard a crack, like a fence rail breaking. Instantly, he knew what had happened–it was at that moment that Spectrum's leg broke. Now his horse was in pain, too. "I'll prob'bly never be able t'ride 'em again," Ted moaned, tears moistening his eyes. "What's gonna' happen to 'em, Rolan'? He'll prob'bly just walk aroun'...just limp aroun' for the rest of his life. Did you bandage 'em up, Rolan'? Did you?" Ted leaned on one painful elbow and pressed anxiously for an answer. "Did you bandage 'em?"

Roland swallowed hard. His face reflected the worst unpleasantness of his life. He looked miserable, and tears preceded words that came painfully slow. "I..." he swallowed hard. "I... , had to..." He sniffed. "I had to shoot 'em, Ted."

For Ted, time stopped! Roland's words felt like a lightening strike went through his body. In painful realization, he opened his mouth as he felt sharp cuts somewhere inside his chest. He sucked in a long, wavering breath. "Noooooooo!" he exploded. "No. No. No. No. No!" he cried as he lifted himself off the bed and hammered sore fists at Roland, only to fall back in a pain that not only racked his body, but now also raked his soul. With a flood of tears running down his cheeks, he whimpered like a dying animal. "No-o-o-o-o-o-o!" he stuttered as he sobbed without shame, the painful outburst shaking his whole body.

Roland continued to sit on the edge of the bed, his body also shaking with sobs. Ma Crockett stood beside the bed, her face wet with tears. "We can bandage his body," she breathed tearfully, "but how we gonna' heal a hurt that goes clear through the heart, all the way to the spirit?" She buried her face in a towel and cried silently.

Empathy and sympathy nudged Roland to reach for Ted's hand and cup it in his as Ma Crockett dropped to her knees beside the bed and stroked Ted's forehead. The tension in the room crested, followed by considerable blowing of noses. Ted lay exhausted and sank into his bed, his unseeing eyes staring at the ceiling, his mind far away. Ma Crocket kissed his forehead and whispered: "I'm sorry, Ted." She stroked his forehead lightly–tender, motherly strokes–before she touched another kiss to his forehead, arose and slowly walked out of the room.

Roland lingered. Taking Ted's hand again, he gave it a brotherly squeeze. "You're gonna'..." he started to whisper, but the sobs started again. "I'll...be back after you rest," he sniffed. At the doorway, he wiped his eyes and inhaled deeply as if wanting to suck in some kind of soothing medicine to heal all the misery in the house.

Ted, now alone, wallowed in his feelings, in his hurt, in his misery. His crying stopped, slowly replaced by remorse and more self-pity. A lot of "if onlys" swirled in his head, but the impact of Spectrum's destruction slammed him to the very depths of despair. Curling up, he felt helpless and hopeless as bitter tears began to flow again. Stabbing agony tortured his body, but grief and anguish swallowed his entire being. He felt that surely this must be what it feels like to die. Forcing his body into a tighter, more painful curl, he buried his face in the pillow and sobbed violently until, exhausted, he fell into merciful sleep.

In the morning, after a restless night, Ted had difficulty separating the dreams and reality that churned in his head. Everything seemed to swirl like it was all mixed by a giant spoon. He lay still, not even sure what his thoughts were. He was only sure that somewhere entangled in his thoughts there was a determination to get Spectrum back. No...oh no! Spectrum was gone! A few teardrops made tiny pools in his eyes as he felt a deep loneliness and a great sense of loss. Soon his despair softened, but it left the tightness in his stomach and the lump in his throat. Although he lay there destroyed by the physical and emotional pain, Ted began feeling a determination, a promise to himself, to replace Spectrum. Through his pain he resolved that, in whatever way, however he could, he would capture the horse he had seen at the lake. Maybe, he thought, he would even name him Spectrum II, or Spectrum 2nd. Ted felt a little better as his misery gave birth to a new dream. It seemed to lessen the aches and the hurt.

In the coming weeks, Ted missed school to allow his body to heal. It did, but not completely, and he still walked slowly and moved stiffly. One day, he and Roland were sitting on stools next to the barn, their backs to the sun. The warmth felt good and dispelled some of the late October chill that had drifted in on an early 'norther'.

"I really miss Spectrum," Ted complained. "Can you tell me where you put 'em?" "That wouldn't do you any good," Roland mused.

Ted turned to face his brother. "Rolan', you think I can get another horse?"

"How?" Roland questioned. "We don't exactly have spare horses runnin' aroun' out here."

Ted chose his words carefully. "I mean one that…that don't belong to nobody."

"Oh, sure," Roland chuckled. "Just go pick one from all the loose horses walkin' aroun' all over the place."

Ted felt a little anger at his brother's joking and he wished Roland could get more serious. "There ***is*** one," he emphasized.

Roland looked seriously at Ted, who had just gained the confidence he needed to tell his brother about the wild horse at the lake. Turning his entire body to face Roland, he could hardly hide the excitement building up in him. "I seen one out by the lake," he began, "even before I went to the Brotchells." His remark reminded him of his folly and he lowered his voice. But instantly, he recovered his excitement. "I seen 'em. Rolan'." Suddenly, a horse galloped into Ted's imagination. "Rolan', you shoulda' seen 'em run!"

"C'mon, Ted," Roland said doubtfully. "There's no loose horse hangin' aroun' out there. Long as we lived here, Pa or me or nobody ever saw one. C'mon, you're makin' this up." He teasingly mussed up Ted's hair, giving the top of his head a brotherly pat. "Maybe you're imaginin' stuff from all the beatin' you took."

"Rolan'!" Ted protested as he got up to leave. His brother's disbelief irritated him and when he turned to face him, Ted looked as though he was about to cry. "I'll show you!" he spouted and huffed off toward the house, although somewhat slowly and stiffly.

The next morning, as the sun was just at the horizon, Ted was on his way–still slowly and stiffly–to the lake. Drawing his coat up around his neck against the cold morning air, he looked up at a flock of geese honking their way across the sky. In the early light, they looked like waving little ghosts floating overhead.

Ted enjoyed the geese which, together with the migrating ducks, arrived every winter like meals on wings sent by nature to feed the Crockett family. Some mornings, Roland–sometimes Ted, too–went to the field to the blind that Roland–and Ted, too–had built. Ted's part had been to pound long stakes into the ground and stretch twine all around, leaving a small opening for the entry. Then, they both collected bundles of maize, which had been harvested and put up in shocks to dry, and leaned them against the twine all around, except for the small opening that was the entry.

Roland–sometimes Ted, too–went out before sunup and scattered newspapers near the blind for decoys, placing clods of dirt on each paper to keep it from blowing away. Then they hid in the blind while the decoys brought the geese close enough so that Roland –sometimes Ted, too–could bag one or two. The shots from Roland's twelve-gage shotgun echoed all over the field.

Ted, however, was allowed to use only the sixteen-gage. Its recoil kicked his shoulder pleasantly and gave him a sense of power. When geese were flying overhead, he would shoot and re-load as fast as he could, but he never was fast enough and the geese would be out of range by the time he was ready for a second shot. Roland almost always fired two shots and sometimes got two geese. Ted was lucky to get one, if any at all.

But the hunt was always fun. Ted even got buck fever sometimes, brought on by the large number of geese flying all around, their honking coming from all directions. When that happened, the excitement gripped him, overcame him, and he fired wildly into the air, not even taking aim, shot after shot as fast as he could. He might shoot five or six times, all out of control, before Roland was able to calm him down. He hardly ever hit any geese during such a lunatic frenzy and faced returning home empty-handed and embarrassed.

The memory revived some of the embarrassment even now as he shuffled toward the lake. But he felt excitement, too, listening to the honking overhead. His mind, however, was more on trying to find the wild horse than on shooting geese. As he reached the lake, a small flock of ducks launched themselves like little missiles, their fast-beating wings whirring like giant hummingbirds.

As dawn erased shadowy outlines of trees and the lake shoreline, Ted searched the area, especially the far side of the lake where he had seen the horse. He strained to hear any sound that might indicate the presence of the wild horse but, except for the ducks and geese, only silence greeted him. He sat down on the bank and peered into the fading blackness of the water. Even though morning was only beginning, he could see reflected on the still surface the first light of the eastern sky, deep as eternity. He felt that if he stepped into the water, he would fall forever. It looked eerie and strange in the early morning,

Suddenly, a noise from the other side of the lake startled him. Ted looked up and his heart began to pound. There, against the dim blackness of the woods, near a strand of misty fog that hung in the air like a chiffon veil, proudly stood his dream. In open mouth wonder, and tingling excitement, he beheld his wild horse.

Locking his eyes on it, he rose slowly, ignoring any pain and, just as slowly, began breathlessly to move along the bank in the direction of the horse. The horse stood alert, majestic and proud, studying Ted, whose contained excitement made his muscles quiver and his legs wobble. Whatever physical pain remained in his body was forgotten as he slowly, purposely, eased toward the animal.

Abruptly, the horse acknowledged his presence with a snort and a shake of its head and trotted off toward the woods, turning from side to side to look back at Ted. At the edge of the woods, where Main Trail looked like a dark tunnel, the horse stopped and turned around, taking another look at Ted. With a snort and a small shake of the head, it whirled around and disappeared into the woods.

Excited beyond endurance, Ted ran toward Main Trail, although stiffly, and paused at the entrance just long enough to beg the sun for more light. Continuing, he fearlessly entered the shadowy woods to follow a horse he could not see, going more by instinct than by sight. Some fear did color his excitement for he had never ventured into the woods this early in the morning. However, as shadows slowly dissolved and the morning sun brightened the world, he was spurred on by excitement and anticipation. He peered through every opening in the underbrush and listened to every sound. Eventually, Main Trail turned into Big Swale, but Ted pressed on, images of the wild horse blotting out any possibility of danger. Slowly, however, disappointment began to replace anticipation.

Searching the space ahead, Ted saw a clearing. The pit of his stomach tightened as he realized that his concentration on the search caused him to ignore his location and he now faced the heart-stopping realization that once more he was at the edge of the Brotchell homestead. He felt that the Brotchells might be out doing their morning chores and he surely did not want to be discovered. He dare not be discovered! The wild horse retreated to the back of his mind as he remembered the mistreatment he had received here not too many days ago. This time, he listened to his good sense. Retreating into the woods, he followed Main Trail back home.

Along the way, his mind pitted the scare of his close encounter at the edge of the Brotchell homestead against continuing the search for the horse. He decided to end the search for now.

Arriving back at the lake, he stopped to re-live what had taken place there earlier. He imagined it as it had been that dawn, with the horse standing alert, powerful, beautiful and looking at him. The pleasure of the memory excited him almost as much as the original scene had. He smiled a knowing, justified smile until the whir of duck wings overhead startled him. Taking a deep breath, he glanced at the ducks zeroing in on the lake. Hopeful, he scanned the whole area just in case the wild horse had returned. Re-living the memory brought a harmony and peace to Ted's mind and he began to hear a melody in his head. Slipping a hand into his pocket, he pulled out his harmonica and triumphantly played his way back to the house.

A warm breakfast awaited him but Ted spoke before he took his first bite. "Rolan', you shoulda' seen the geese out there this mornin'. Ducks, too."

"What were you doin' out there so early?"

"Oh ... just wanted to be out there."

"Yeah!" Roland's reaction reflected a degree of knowing.

"When does goose season open, Rolan'? We gonna' hunt some?"

"Haven't looked. But it don't matter none."

Finishing breakfast, Ted sought out his father and found him enjoying the back porch, rocking in the chair he had made for himself years ago. His head rested deep in a pillow and his huge body pressed back in the chair. Bulky arms extended away from the armrests as though accepting the warmth of the morning sun.

"G'mornin', Pa," Ted greeted as he positioned a chair close to his father. "You feelin' better?"

"Yeah ... comin' along O.K." He started rocking with a little more enthusiasm. "You still look a little black n' blue…you feelin' alright?"

"Yeah, Pa. Still hurts a little some."

The porch suddenly grew so quiet Ted could almost hear the sunshine.

I recollect you had somethin' to tell me." Pa Crockett gave Ted time to think. "Remember?"

Ted remembered. He recalled the night by his father's bedside, late, when he couldn't sleep–the day his father had been shot. That, however, was not what he wanted to talk about and he searched for the right words. "If…ah "… . He sat thinking it over but his father's hawk-like gaze demanded that he continue. "Pa, there's a wild horse out in the woods behind the lake."

Pa Crockett stopped rocking and relaxed his body. A hint of a smile pulled at his lips.

"Ted, you always did have a good imagination, but this is big." He rocked a few times in silence. "I walked them woods a hundred times. Never saw a wild horse there." He rocked some more. "What did he look like?"

Ted was having trouble hiding his disappointment at his father's disbelief. First Roland, now his father. He did not want to answer but the memory of the horse, the picture in his mind of him standing there in the dawn, encouraged Ted to go on. "Pa, I really seen 'em," he began timidly. "I seen 'em this mornin'." His self-confidence grew. "An' I heard 'em once before and seen 'em in the evenin'. That was the time I came home late–an' he was like a shadow in the dark, Pa. You shoulda' seen 'em run!" Ted was coming alive, starting to talk faster. "But this mornin', there was light an' I seen he was brown, an' he was powerful, an' he stood there lookin' at me...an' he was beautiful, Pa!" Ted beamed a smile at his father. "You shoulda' seen 'em, Pa. Shoulda' seen 'em run!"

Pa Crockett took a deep breath and exhaled loudly while he rocked in silent thought, as was his habit. He rocked this way for what seemed like a long time to Ted, and Ted sat nervously and anxiously shifting in his chair, waiting for his father's reaction. Finally, Pa Crockett offered no more than a warning. "If there is a wild horse out there, you leave 'em alone. No need you getting' trampled again." There was a lightness in his warning just as there was in his reaction to Ted's story.

Ted got up and threw back a disappointed "O.K. Pa" as he surrendered his father back to the sunshine. In his room, he sat on his bed, depressed, and tried to sort out his feelings. Neither his father nor Roland believed him. He feared disobeying his father, but somehow and some way he would have to catch the wild horse. He would show them that what he had seen was real, not just his imagination. Lying there, he began making plans for the capture.

Ted didn't go back to the lake for a few days. He made plans, however, even while daydreaming in the classroom at school, and had decided to build a capture pen. In his mind, he worked out its location, the way to build it, position it–there were many things to consider for the capturing and holding of a wild animal many times his size. But he could not decide how to entice the horse into the trap. In his resourceful way, he had noted items that he could scrounge from around the homestead: rope, wire, posts, boards. Now, if he could just work out a way to make the horse enter the trap.

Once more at the lake, he sat on the bank and folded his arms across his upright knees. Resting his chin on his folded forearms, he peered into the water as though expecting the answer to appear in the ripples. His mind worked feverishly on the last problem. Not even a skimmer bird making a long line across the surface of the water distracted him. Though his eyes followed the bird, his mind did not see it and the bird flew off into the sky alone.

Ted got up and wandered toward the place where the wild horse had stood a few days before. He needed to study this area for the placement of the trap, and walking around there might give him some ideas. But soon the whole thing began to look like an overwhelming task and he began to doubt his ability to capture such a large animal. He questioned his method - wire and rope stretched between wobbly posts would not hold a wild horse. This was not like building a blind from which to shoot geese. Maybe if he used some of the trees for posts. But then he would have to clear the underbrush, and the trees may not be in the right places.

Overcome by the enormity of the task he had assigned himself, Ted kicked at a clod of dirt. His obsession with the horse had filled his mind during the past few days, even interfering with schoolwork. His teacher had talked to him about a visit with his parents concerning his lack of attention in class. Inhaling a deep breath, he exhaled a swift sigh, picked up a clod of dirt and hurled it at a tree trunk. Feeling totally overcome, almost defeated before he even started, he began a gloomy amble toward the house.

Dejected, he intercepted Roland walking briskly across the front yard. "Whatcha' doin', Rolan'?" he asked, picking up the pace to keep up with his brother.

"Need to fix a hole in the pig pen. Ma said a pig ate a chicken that got into the pen yesterday. "

Ted had to take an extra step to keep up. "Rolan', I been thinkin' about that horse out at the lake." By now, the horse seemed to have been assigned the area of the lake as his home.

"You have?" Roland smiled but didn't even break his stride as he glanced at Ted. "What did you think?"

Rolan', you think you could help me catch 'em?" Ted surprised himself with his directness.

Roland stopped in his tracks. Ted walked ahead a few steps, stopped and turned around to face his brother.

"Could you', Rolan'?" The face beaming up at Roland expressed all the longing Ted felt inside. The desire to catch the horse dispelled any timidity that may otherwise have been present in such a request. "Would you'?" he pleaded earnestly.

Roland resumed his walk but he was thoughtful and walked slower than before.

Ted stuck with him like a pestering fly. "Could you?" he insisted.

"Ted, the only thing you're goin' to catch is trouble," Roland replied impatiently. "There's no horse out there."

All the rejection from Roland and his father burst out of its banks inside Ted. "How do you know?" he shouted emphatically. "You didn't even go out there to look. You don't even care if I seen one, or what I seen. You an' Pa, none of you care." His outburst trailed off into the subdued, whimpering voice of hurt feelings that he always tried to keep to himself. "Nobody believes me."

They were now almost at the pig pen and Roland stopped. "Tell ya' what, Ted," he proposed, "you help me with this job and then we'll go have a look."

Ted's outlook changed immediately, his spirits leaping out of the hole of depression where he had stuffed them. "O.K.!" he chimed. "Whatcha' want me t'do?"

"Go to the workshop an' bring a hammer," Roland ordered as he examined the fence. "An' some nails."

Ted bounced off, as best as he could, in the direction of the workshop and quickly returned with the hammer and nails. After watching Roland, always so resourceful, fix the hole in the fence, he led him to the far side of the lake where the wild horse lived. At least, in Ted's mind, it did.

"I seen 'em right here, Rolan'. I was over there sittin' on the bank," he said, pointing.

Roland looked around but saw no evidence of Ted's horse. "He went into the woods right there." Ted pointed excitedly at Main Trail, "an' I followed 'em but couldn't find 'em." He carefully avoided telling Roland about wandering so close to the Brotchell home.

"Weeell, I don't know," Roland said thoughtfully. "Really cain't tell nothin'." He started to walk back toward the house. "You sure of what you saw? You did say it was kinda' dark."

"Shucks, Rolan', I know what I seen." Ted's elation began to subside, and he started to follow his brother. They both strolled in silence.

Rounding the lake, Roland stopped to pick up a stick, about three feet long, and eyed a patch of damp, soft clay nearby. "Bet I can sling farther than you," he challenged.

Ted was not really interested in clay slinging right now, being depressed by his brother's disbelief, but he always liked competition and didn't wait long to accept the challenge. Without a word, both boys reached down and scooped up a handful of moist clay. "You first," Ted said as he molded the clay into a compact ball. The point was to use the stick as a whip to see how far they could throw a ball of clay affixed to it. They engaged in this contest now and then, but sometimes Ted would sling clay alone, either just lobbing the balls or throwing at birds that happened by. There never was any danger to the birds as the accuracy of the throw was not very good.

By now, Roland had kneaded his clay into a solid ball and had impaled it onto the stick. "Watch this!" he bragged as he reared back and heaved the stick forward. There was a pleasant 'pop' as the clay ball separated from the stick and traveled in an arc over the lake. It hit the ground a short distance from the shore on the other side. "Beat that," he challenged.

Ted, grinning at the opportunity, took the stick from his brother, impaled a fresh ball onto it and reared back. "Here goes!" he exclaimed as he swung the stick forward over his head, exerting, through some lingering pain, his mightiest effort. There was the familiar 'pop' as the ball left the stick, then arced over the lake and splashed in the water just short of the opposite bank.

"That was a good one," Roland encouraged as he found another stick and affixed another ball.

The boys now engaged in a frenzy of laughter and enjoyment as they threw ball after ball just for the fun. They laughed extra hard when an unfortunate bird had to dive almost to the ground to avoid being hit by one of the balls. That looked so comical that Ted couldn't resist taking credit for the throw. The game continued for several minutes, stopping only after the boys grew tired of the sport. The event dispelled tension and once more Ted felt close to his brother. They compared their throws and laughed as they squatted at the water's edge and washed their hands. The joking and giggling continued all the way back to the house. Their spirits were never better.

The next day, Ted was at the woodpile absorbed in preparing to chop firewood. But when the snort came from the direction of the lake, he straightened up as though he were a wound up spring. Once again, his heart skipped as he spotted the wild horse, standing alert and powerful, and attentively studying Ted. He was about a hundred yards away, just standing and looking at him. Ted's impulse was to shout for Roland to come and look…no, he should try to approach the horse…no, he should run to the house and get Roland and his father…no, he should…heck! What should he do?" The indecision paralyzed him into simply staring back at the horse, so beautiful, like a magnificent statue.

Not knowing how to take advantage of this opportunity, Ted gave in to excitement and began to move, slowly, toward the horse, step after gentle step like the fluid motion of a cat stalking a bird. His body quivered with excitement; his heart pounded. He almost didn't breathe. Suddenly, the statue came to life, snorted and trotted back around to the far side of the lake, stopping at the entrance to Main Trail. There, it turned to study Ted some more. Ted could not restrain himself. On impulse, he bolted, as best as he could, after the horse which simply turned and vanished into the woods. Just as he had before, Ted followed as swiftly as he could, listening for any sound the horse might make. Approaching Big Swale, he slowed his step, then stopped in disbelief. There he was, in the clearing! Crouching down low, he crept closer, staying hidden behind bushes.

The thrill was breathlessly intoxicating as he crept closer and slowly raised his head to peer over the bushes. The horse was almost at center stage, nibbling at tufts of grass. Nothing on earth could duplicate the thrill of that moment. Ted remained hidden behind the bushes, hypnotized, and watched the horse nibble grass, enjoy it, then step to the next tuft.

Suddenly, the peaceful scene was shattered as three men dashed out of the woods from three different points, yelling and circling ropes overhead as they tried to surround the horse.

"Brotchells!" Ted sneered under his breath. "Them stinkin' Brotchells!" Fury quickly replaced the elation Ted had felt just moments before. He watched in helpless frustration as the Brotchells hollered and shouted and had fun trying to lasso the horse. Ted watched as the horse trotted in a circle within the triangle of men. Suddenly, at full gallop, it dashed between two of them, raising puffs of dust as each hoof dug into the earth and, in mere moments, disappeared into the woods. Ted wanted to clap and cheer at the happy outcome, but he only clapped lightly–to himself–and cheered quietly–to himself. He was grateful for the horse's escape.

The Brotchells laughed and jabbered and slapped their legs and each other in the sickening aftermath of their twisted fun. They laughed and enjoyed themselves at the expense of 'his horse'. Winding down from their game, their fun almost exhausted, they began walking across the clearing toward the far side. They were still talking and chuckling when they, like the horse, disappeared into the woods.

Ted was flush with anger, feeling again the sharp pains from the Brotchell's mean spirit. As he stared into the silent stage of Big Swale, now cleared of all actors, he became more determined than ever to catch the horse, if for no other reason than to keep it out of the hands of the Brotchells. He felt powerless against them but the stubbornness and grit of a Goliath gripped him and he resolved that they must never have their fun with *his* horse again. Picking himself up, he walked with determined steps back down Main Trail, absorbed in the planning of the capture.

5

The Plot

Ted and Roland sat in the barn shucking corn, always an unpleasant chore. The corn, with many of the kernels scarcely more than empty hulls–the substance inside having been eaten by weevils–would feed the chickens; the shuck, carefully saved in baskets, would feed the cows. But the activity released clouds of powdery, itching dust. Ted always hated this chore. In addition to the dust, the edges of the shuck could be sharp, sometimes cutting his fingers. He wondered how the cows could chew on it and not cut up their mouths.

After the shucking, the ears of corn were run through the shelling machine that separated the kernels from the cob, a process that produced more itching dust. The kernels were collected in buckets for the evening feeding of the chickens. The corncobs were of no use although sometimes a cow would chew on one. Ted never understood why since the cobs appeared so dry and tasteless.

Now, as Ted examined one of the cobs he had just shelled, a sense of play came over him. He broke the cob in half and found three chicken wing feathers, which were plentiful in the barn area. He then stuck the feathers into the soft center at the end of the broken cob. The result was a crude, but practical, shuttlecock.

"Hey, Rolan', look!" he called as he threw it into the air and watched it spin to earth.

"That's nothin'," Roland bragged as he broke a cob in half and constructed his own shuttlecock. "Watch this!"

In very little time, a contest ensued. The point was to see who threw higher and whose shuttlecock spun the fastest on its descent. As in most of the boys' contests, this one became such a frenzy that it ended up not being a competition at all. Instead, the boys hollered and laughed and threw until the sport got old and they felt exhausted. Collapsing on the ground in laughter, they lay on their backs spread out on the ground, their stomachs and chests jiggling with dying laughter.

"I almost hit yours a coupla' times."

"Not a chance! Mine was divin' to get away."

"Yeah, but you lost a feather an' yours kinda' wobbled in for a crash. Mine twirled down a lot better."

After a few more minutes of laughter and banter, the boys sat up. Roland picked up a tiny dirt clod and lobbed it onto Ted's head. Ted enjoyed this good time with his brother and he took advantage of what he saw as an opportunity to talk to his brother about the horse. "Rolan', remember me talkin' about that wild horse?"

"I thought that was settled, that there is nothin' out there."

"There really is, Rolan'. I seen 'em again yesterday." There was an impatience in Ted's voice. "I was at the woodpile an' I seen 'em over by the lake."

"Aw, c'mon, Ted. It was prob'ly a cow," Roland joked.

"Honest, Rolan'! An' I tracked 'em to Big Swale! An' I watched them Brotchells try to catch 'em! But he got away! But them Brotchells just had fun scarin' 'em an' everythin'." Ted paused to think. "I hate them Brotchells," he concluded, stressing the word 'hate' so forcefully that it jerked his body forward.

During the silence that followed, Roland got up and took the lead in returning to the task of shucking corn. Soon, each boy was sitting in his own little dust cloud.

Ted finally spoke, carefully choosing his words. "Rolan', if we look one more time an' you see there really is a horse out there, would you help me catch 'em?" He stopped working and looked seriously at Roland.

A smile teased the corners of Roland's mouth as he got up and tossed the last ear of corn into the bucket, slapping dust off himself.

"Huh, Rolan', would you?" Ted strained a pleading face up at his brother.

"Well," Roland said thoughtfully, still dusting himself, "we'll look one more time. But," he added quickly, "if we don't find anythin', if there's no sign that there's a horse out there, that will be the end of it, O.K? I ain't chasin' after your make-believe stuff again."

Ted blasted off his seat with an enthusiastic "O.K." and, dusting himself off, followed Roland out of the barn, his arms hugging a basket full of shuck and his face grinning victory.

At the cow pen, Ted emptied the basket of shuck over the fence, set the basket down and pointed toward the lake, all in one motion. "Over there, Rolan'. That's where I seen 'em." He hurried ahead and stopped on the spot where he had seen the wild horse standing the day before. "Look, Rolan'! These tracks! You can see where he started to run…right here!" He looked over the ground with growing excitement. "An' he ran that way," he pointed, "around the lake and into the woods at Main Trail." He hastened in that direction.

Roland followed without saying a word, but glanced over the ground at the evidence.

At the edge of the woods, he spoke. "Looks like there was a horse here aw'right. But a wild one? Ted, would a wild one come this close to the house?" He pointed in the direction of the woodpile.

Ted ignored the question. "He went into the woods right here where we are."

Completely engrossed in the experience, he talked much faster than his slow, thoughtful way. "Let's go look at Big Swale, Rolan' ," he proposed and, without waiting for his brother's agreement, bounced into the woods and down Main trail. Excitement carried him quickly to Big Swale and he arrived well ahead of Roland.

"This is where Pa got shot," Roland observed.

"Yeah! Strange, ain't it," Ted remarked as he led the way into the clearing. "Over there is where them Brotchells tried to catch 'em." Ted ran to the spot. "Look, Rolan'," he exclaimed, "look at all the hoof marks! An' here's footprints from them Brotchells!" Ted's excitement bubbled over as both boys bent over to study the ground.

"Ted," Roland mused," looks like you really saw somethin' here. But did the horse really look wild? You sure?"

Ted spoke with conviction. "Aw, sure! He's wild aw'right. You shoulda' seen 'em fightin' them Brotchells." Ted's active animation enlivened the scene. "He raised on his hin' legs an' he pawed the air an' snorted an' whinnied! It was a real fight." He paused, re-living the scene. "Then he zipped between two of them Brotchells an' got away into the woods." Pausing again just for a second, he concluded with the pride of ownership in his voice. "I was so proud of that horse. You shoulda' seen 'em', Rolan' ."

Roland paced around slowly. "If the horse was really wild, he would not let the Brotchells sneak up on 'em an' surround 'em. Wild horses are smart an' alert."

"They musta' been real quiet. I didn't hear nothin' til them brotchells came crashin' out of the woods." Ted tried to rescue whatever bit of conviction Roland had up to this point.

"The next time you see 'em," Roland tossed back as he started to return to Main Trail, "don't follow 'em. Come get me 'cause I wanna' have a look. I wanna' see what he looks like."

"Rolan' ," Ted pleaded desperately, "you can see there's a horse here. Cain't you help me catch 'em?" He caught up to his brother and searched his face for a sign of agreement.

"Cain't you?"

"How you gonna' do that?' Roland questioned as they neared the edge of the woods.

"You don't just walk up an' throw a rope on a wild horse…if he's really wild."

"We can figger out a way, Rolan'." Ted now felt that Roland was on his side. "Maybe we can make a corral, or corner 'em an' rope 'em," Ted pleaded earnestly. "Or set a trap." He was running out of suggestions, but he tried to keep the momentum going. "Or chase 'em down an' rope 'em." Now he really was out of ideas.

Roland chuckled. "Boy, you're serious, aintcha'?"

The boys entered Main Trail and proceeded silently in single file. Now and then, their shirts or trousers rasped in protest as brush or low tree branches scraped against them. "What if we put out some corn to lure 'em into a trap?" Ted suggested as he dodged a small branch swatting at him, cocked by Roland's passage ahead of him.

"Guess we could try that," Roland agreed halfheartedly as he cocked another branch. Ted suddenly felt a rush of victory, taking Roland's remark as a commitment to help.

"Where we gonna' catch 'em, Rolan'?" He suddenly shifted the focus of the capture to Roland, giving his brother credit for greater experience and wisdom.

"Well ... " Roland began but walked on in silence. After a short distance, he added:

"Shucks, Ted, I don't know!" They were now coming out of the woods near the lake, and Roland continued. "Maybe if we got 'em over there, where the fence goes into the lake. At least, we'd have 'em cornered on two sides."

"Yeah!" Ted burst out excitedly. "An' we can stretch some wire or rope to make it like a pen!"

The two boys studied the area. It was some distance away on the southern side of the lake where one leg of the barbed wire fence enclosing the pasture entered into the lake.

"We could make a trail of corn from here to there," Roland offered.

The boys felt drawn to the area and walked briskly around the lake to the fence, stopping at the water's edge and looking back at what would become the capture area.

"We can hide over there," Ted pointed confidently, "in that clump of bushes." There was a pause while the rest of the plan formed. "You think we can rope 'em?"

"Won't be easy."

"I got it!" Ted almost shouted. "When he's way at the water and fence, we can run a circle 'round 'em with a rope an' rope off his escape."

"A single rope fence ain't gonna' hold a wild horse," Roland assured. "If he's really wild, that is. Maybe we oughta' just forget the whole thing."

"No, Rolan', we can catch 'em," Ted pleaded "C'mon, Rolan', let's try!"

"Well…" Roland's commitment seemed to waver. "But we better not let Pa know what we're doin'."

With Roland on his side again, Ted felt the excitement of the coming adventure.

"Let's do it tomorrow mornin'," he proposed.

"I think the best we'll be able to do is try to corner 'em." Roland spoke thoughtfully as he looked over the landscape again. "But he can easily get by us if he wants to, just like you say he did the Brotchells." After a pause, he continued. "Guess tryin' to rope 'em is the best we'll be able to do."

"Let's get some corn ready," Ted suggested, already imagining the roped horse in his hands. As the boys walked around the lake toward the barn, Ted asked: "You think I'll be able to ride 'em soon?" He dreamed out loud. "How long you think it will take to break 'em, Rolan'?"

"Whoa, there, not so fast," Roland cautioned. "We ain't even caught 'em yet. An' breakin' 'em...boy! That is, if Pa would even let us keep 'em."

They walked on in silence. Ted feared that Roland might change his mind again.

The next morning, the Crockett household was jarred awake by a very loud thunderclap. Hail and huge drops of rain pounded the tin roof of the house like hundreds of hammers as gusts of wind moaned and slammed into the side of the house. Normally, such heavy rain on the roof relaxed Ted and made him sleepy. He had even positioned his bed so that his head snuggled near the ceiling, where the roof slanted downward. There, the melody of the storm so near his head usually lulled him to sleep, even when it happened during the day.

But this morning, the wind-driven downpour only brought disappointment. In frustration, Ted threw the covers off himself. Lying exposed to the chill, he began to shiver as the cold air nipped at his body. In spite of the cold, however, he slipped out of bed and crossed the wood floor to the window to peer into the darkness outside. A flash of lightening illuminated puddles of water on the ground. Wiggly rivers of water streamed down the outside of the window drenched by a sheet of rain. Shivering, Ted hastened back to the warmth of the bed, pulling the blanket up to his ears.

Roland stirred. "Bad out there, huh?" he mumbled but remained snug under the covers.

"Yeah," Ted answered sadly. He thought about the wild horse, somewhere out there in the cold rain. But he only wondered and did not really worry for he understood that animals in the wild knew how to take care of themselves. Even now, his horse was probably lying behind a thicket to protect itself from the cold wind. Ted closed his eyes and listened to the rain. It was like music. He began to visualize himself sitting proud and tall on the horse's back. He imagined how his horse would respond to his commands. Just a light kick of his heels into the horse's side would unleash the power of a gallop unmatched by any horse in the area, including all the Brotchell horses. *Especially* the Brotchell horses. He might even race at full gallop through their yard, hollering and shouting, for they could never catch him. With such pictures racing through his mind, Ted drifted off to sleep.

When he awoke, pale daylight beckoned through the window. Rain still pounded the house, but the strength of the storm had moved on with the cold front that had brought it. Everyone else was still asleep, something normal on a morning like this. Usually, he would sleep late too, but this morning, he could sleep no more. Getting out of bed, he quickly put on cold clothes, shivering all the while, especially when the cold shirt wrapped around his chest. He hated a cold shirt on a cold morning.

Stealing quietly down the stairs, he made his way to the potbelly stove in the middle of the living room. Opening the ash compartment at the bottom, he ladled out the ashes from the last fire into a bucket. He tried to do it quietly, but the clank of metal on metal was hard to keep quiet and he may as well have been standing in the middle of the living room and hammering on a sheet of tin. At least, that's the way it sounded to him.

But he managed to clean out the ashes without waking anyone, or so he thought. After wadding up some newspaper and placing it into the belly of the stove, he put kindling sticks on top of it and added three logs from the stack on the porch. It was something like building a campfire, except it was inside. Lighting the paper, he clanked the door shut and made some adjustments to the air vents. Then he stepped back to wait for his reward–the gift of heat. The small fire inside the potbelly stove whispered at first, then came to life with a roar, engulfing paper, sticks and logs. Ted kept touching the side of the stove, feeling the heat increasing. Finally, it became too hot to touch. Turning his back to the stove, he absorbed the radiating heat.

Just then, Ma and Pa Crockett entered the room, grateful for the growing warmth.

Some rumbling noises even came from upstairs, a sign that Roland was getting up too. It seemed that firing up the potbelly stove was a sign for everyone to get up.

"Some norther out there," a bundled up Ma Crockett observed on her way to the kitchen. Pa Crockett pulled a chair up to the stove and sat down as Roland arrived, yawning. The potbelly stove was now radiating heat like the sun and Pa Crockett, Roland and Ted huddled around it like planets.

"Not much to do today," Ted muttered, resigned to staying indoors. He didn't like these wintry days. Especially today! His plans to capture the wild horse were blown away by the norther. "Wish at least the rain would stop," he muttered again, mostly to himself. No one answered.

By noon, the rain had stopped, but the wind continued to blow. Ted bundled up, slipped on rubber boots and, with Roland, ventured outdoors to tend to the livestock and the chickens, normally a morning chore. But before proceeding, Ted took time to study the lake area. Huge flocks of blackbirds flew around like propelled clouds. They blackened the haystacks, the pasture and the field like dark, moving blankets.

"Look at all them blackbirds behind the cowshed," Roland observed.

"Bet I get one before you do," Ted challenged.

The boys made a quick trip back to the house to get BB guns. Then they crept quietly into the cowshed. Taking aim through the holes and cracks in the wall, they popped their BB guns over and over at the rolling blanket of birds. There really was no danger to the birds as the BB guns were not very accurate, although occasionally they did hit one. Now and then, as though on some signal, the birds rose like a black, smoky cloud only to alight a short distance away and continue the feverish search for food.

Returning to the house after completing their chores, the boys left their boots in the mud room, which still had some mud on the floor from the last rain. Sometimes the slippery goo challenged the boys' balance as they teetered and hopped to avoid fresh mud. Finally, in socks, they walked carefully so as not to track mud into the main part of the house.

A wave of warmth greeted them as they entered the living room. The potbelly stove was very generous with its heat as Pa Crocket fed it another log. He stoked the coals, urging the red ashes to fire up and the burned up ashes to fall through the grate to the basin below. It was everyone's duty to keep the fire burning during the day but, during the night, the potbelly stove stood alone and spent its fire. By morning, the house was cold again. Almost always, either Ted or Roland were the fire starters in the morning.

Sunday morning, the road leading to town was muddy and slippery from the rain. That meant not going to church for it was too difficult for Pa Crockett to keep the car from slipping into the ditch. It also meant for Ted that there would be no teasing smile exchange with Wanda, a thought that produced a ripple of loneliness. But worst of all, he could not pursue any activity around the lake because of the mud. Ted didn't like the idea of staying indoors, especially when he had a horse to catch.

On Monday and Tuesday, the muddy road was dry enough to allow cautious transportation to school. By Wednesday, the ground was still soft but dry and the norther had surrendered its cold to the warmth of the sun, lingering only as a mildly chilling breeze. Immediately after coming home from school, Ted was at the lake examining deep hoof prints in the soft earth. He followed the meandering track to the edge of the woods. The excitement that had been cooled by the norther was rekindled as he re-examined the junction of the lake and fence where he and Roland planned to catch the horse.

Looking over the area, he focused on the spot where Main Trail entered the woods.

"Hey!" he exclaimed to himself, "maybe we can catch 'em there!" He hastened toward the trail.

"Maybe we can hang a noose over the trail," he mumbled to him self again, "an' when his head goes through... ." Excitement and anticipation peaked as he hurried back toward the house. He found Roland at the edge of the field working the posthole digger, digging a grave for two chickens he had found dead, probably drownings from the heavy rain. "Rolan'!" he exclaimed breathlessly, "I know how we can catch the horse easy!" Between breaths, he explained his plan about the noose at the entrance of Main Trail. "Whatcha' think, Rolan'? Think it'll work?"

Roland remained quiet as he kicked the dead chickens into the hole and scooted dirt back into it. "Might work," he answered causually. Stomping the dirt down into the filled hole, he continued. "except if he's walkin' and the noose ain't pulled just right over his neck, we might rope 'em around his belly. Then we'd be in real trouble cause he's run off trailin' the rope."

"We can try, Rolan'," Ted implored. "We can do it." "Let's try it, Rolan'. Help me catch 'em," he pleaded.

Roland was slow to commit. "We better have a look at the trail," he offered. Putting the post hole digger into the tool shed on the way, he accompanied Ted to the lake and around to where Main Trail entered the woods. He examined the layout. "I dunno," he rubbed his chin. "I think first we better try cornering 'em over there." Both boys cast a look toward the lake and fence junction.

"You think that's better?"

"Yeah. This here looks too dangerous." Roland was already walking back toward the house as he spoke.

"Can we try Saturday mornin'?" Ted asked impatiently.

"Guess we may as well. I really doubt we'll catch 'em ... especially if he's really wild."

"But we can try," Ted emphasized. "An' he really is wild! I seen 'em when he was fightin' them Brotchells."

"Yeah, yeah," Roland retorted with a hint of impatience. "We'll see on Saturday." Ted skipped a step and hopped another at the joy of Roland's commitment.

Friday evening, as the sun, low behind the trees, was about to kiss the edge of the earth, Ted was at the lake placing corn in a line from Main Trail to the area of the planned capture. He had stealthily snitched corn from the barn, making sure not to be seen by his father, who certainly would have judged this to be a waste of corn. He measured out just enough corn to entice the horse to keep going: a little pile here, a half an ear there. "I hope there's some left in the mornin'," he muttered to himself. "You squirrels and rabbits leave this alone." Other creatures, like rats, would also claim their portion during the night. Before leaving the lake, he glanced back at the trail of corn and visualized the horse already there.

Returning to the house, he joined Ma Crockett sitting on the porch step. "What a beautiful sunset," she observed.

"Sure is, Ma."

Together, they watched in silence as the western sky blazed red, graduated to orange, yellow and chartreuse, then faded to a darkening crimson and pink, and finally surrendered the evening to the emerging stars. "No artist could paint that," Ma Crockett mused, almost religiously.

"Yeah, Ma, it looked good." Ted enjoyed watching sunsets, and he took pleasure in the colors.

"Ted, what do you think about when you see something like that ... like the sunset." Ted was slow to answer. "Sometimes, Ma," he turned his gaze skyward, "sometimes I wonder what there would be if there was nothin'."

"How can you think that? How can you think nothin'?"

"I mean, if there was no earth, no sun, no stars ... nothin'. What would there be? Just space? Or maybe space wouldn't be there either 'cause there would be nothin' to be in it. "

"That's more thinkin' than I have brains for, Ted." Ma Crockett followed Ted's gaze skyward. "What would you do if there was nothin'?"

Ted thought for a moment. "Guess I wouldn't do nothin'. Guess I wouldn't even be here." Ted sometimes wondered about things like that, but he almost never talked to anyone about them.

Ma Crockett looked at her son. "But there would still be God."

"Yeah, but ... God is nothin'."

"Ted!"

"I mean, He's a spirit, an' in that way He's nothin'."

Ma Crockett looked at the darkening western sky, where the planet Venus was brightening up for the night. "But ... God would have to be somewhere, even as a spirit. Where do you think He would be if there was nothin'?"

Ted thought deeply. "Guess He would have to be someplace else," he said slowly, thinking on each word. "Ma, what do you think is out there ... on the other side of space?"

The silence of the universe itself descended upon mother and son as their faces remained turned toward the heavens. Ma Crockett studied the stars for a long moment. "Ted, you just think about that. I don't know an' I'm gettin' cold. You goin' inside?"

"Think I'll stay here a bit longer, Ma."

"It's gettin' chilly," she said just before she disappeared into the house.

Darkness claimed the night as Ted continued to sit and watch the western sky struggle with the remnants of a faint glow. Leaning back on his elbows, he looked straight up. In just a few short moments, the glowing band of stars that make up the Milky Way, the bright evening star, the millions of other stars filling the overhead canopy–all disappeared in the mind that tried to imagine the nothingness of the universe. In their place, a horse, as real as life, raced across the heavens, stretching long hind legs as they completed their thrust, and forelegs reaching for the next point of contact. The vision held for only a few seconds. "Cain't wait 'til mornin' ," he whispered to himself. "Cain't wait!" With anticipation of the following morning gripping him, he got up and, before entering the house, glanced skyward, then toward the lake. In this glowing moment, Ted Crockett smiled a happy smile.

6

The Capture

The next morning, Ted awoke on cue. It was early. Dawn was still over the horizon and he lay in bed waiting its arrival. His mind, however, was already at the lake.

He dreamed his dream as morning grew brighter. Soon, growing impatient, he got up and looked out the window to see familiar shapes becoming visible, and decided the time had arrived to prepare for the morning's adventure. "Rolan', wake up." He patted his brother on the shoulder. "Time to get up."

Roland raised his head and looked around with half-closed eyes. "Aw, shucks, Ted," he mumbled as he slammed his head back onto the pillow.

"C'mon, Rolan', get up," Ted pleaded, his excitement filling the room. "We're gonna' catch the wild horse today! We'll be late."

"Sure," Roland mumbled as he readjusted his pillow.

"C'mon, Rolan' ," Ted pleaded again.

After more prodding from Ted, Roland sleepily, reluctantly and slowly inched out of bed without a word and, just as slowly, put on his clothes. Ted, on the other hand, zipped into his–never mind that they were cold. After more coaxing from Ted, the boys crept silently down the stairs, past the closed door of their parents' room, and out the door. A blast of chilled air greeted them and they both buttoned up their jackets.

Dawn was on its way to sunrise when Ted and Roland, ropes in hand, made their way to the lake. Their shoes picked up some of the wet soil, damp from the morning dew.

"We better go slow," Roland whispered as they passed by the woodpile.

"Look!" Ted whispered excitedly.

The boys stopped and peered across the lake where the growing morning light revealed a horse, head down, feeding on the com.

"Is that the wild horse?" Roland whispered.

"Yeah! That's 'em!" Ted gushed with excitement even though he could not be sure.

Squinting at the shadowy form, he added, "If there was more light, I could see 'em better."

"You mean you don't know if that's the wild one?"

"That's gotta' be 'em," Ted reassured.

Roland had a moment of impatience and doubt but presented a plan anyway. "Let's go to the edge of the woods an' circle aroun' so we'll be between him and the trail."

Ted felt jittery with excitement as he followed Roland, hunched over, to the woods.

He paid no attention to the dew wetting his jacket as he brushed past branches laden with dewdrops. Roland signaled a halt when they reached the opening to Main Trail. He pointed at the ground where fresh hoof prints in the damp earth proved the recent passage of the horse. In the distance, the horse continued to follow the trail of com, seemingly unaware of the boys.

Roland whispered: "Let's creep slowly, together, toward 'em." He paused, studying the plan. "When we get close, let's split up. But go slow. An' here, hold out this ear of corn toward 'em when you get close."

"How are we gonna' get that close," Ted pondered. "Maybe we can try talkin' to 'em," he volunteered, not even thinking that one doesn't just sneak up and talk a wild horse into anything.

"O.K. But wait 'til we're close. We may never have a chance to throw a rope on 'em."

The boys began a slow, hunched over creep toward the horse, keeping their eyes on it like a bobcat sneaking up on prey. When they had gone about half the distance, the horse raised its head to investigate the intrusion. There were scratches visible on its rump and a few on its side. Ted had not seen these, never having been this close to the horse before.

The horse became agitated and began walking around nervously as the boys separated, moved apart a few feet, and continued to advance at a very slow pace, holding out the ears of corn as offerings.

"Here, boy. Easy there." Roland initiated the conversation.

Ted suffered from such overwhelming excitement that it was a painful challenge for him to proceed calmly. "Here you go, falla'. Come get your corn." Ted's hand shook; his knees wobbled. Here he was, after tolerating the disbelief of his father and Roland, after weeks of dreaming; here he was, about to take possession of his horse.

"Stay calm," Roland cautioned, noticing Ted's panting and fluster.

"C'mon, boy, come get it," the boys kept repeating. "Here you go. Come get it. C'mon, boy." They kept advancing.

The horse suddenly stopped pacing and, with ears and head at the alert, stood and observed the boys. A snort signaled his alarm. Roland and Ted continued their slow advance. "Here, boy. Come get it," they encouraged, holding out the corn. "Come on, boy, come on." The horse stepped nervously. "Here you go. Easy there." The horse snorted, standing tall and alert, studying the boys. "C'mon, Here you go." The horse stepped nervously again, seeming not to know whether to follow the urge to run or the urge to accept the offering of food and friendship.

"Get your corn. C'mon" The boys were now close. A sense of anxiety, nervousness and tension bounced back and forth between boys and horse. "Here you go."

The horse stopped his agitated movements, snorted and nervously faced the boys, now only a few yards away. They stopped, holding out the corn.

"Here you go, boy. Here's your corn," they encouraged. "Easy there. Here you go."

They continued the soothing invitation, trying to stay calm - a real task for Ted.

The horse released an excited breath, just short of a snort, shook its head slightly and took a step forward.

"C'mon, get your corn. Good horse. Now get your corn."

Another step. Another nervous breath.

"C'mon, Here you go."

Step - pause - step.

"C'mon, get your corn. Good horse"

Another gush of breath, hesitation, and a final step brought the horse and corn within reach. Cautiously stretching its neck and slowly reaching out it head, the horse leaned forward in a long stretch, claiming its prize - the ear of com held by Roland.

"Don't move, Ted," Roland cautioned in a whisper.

"That's the way. Easy, now. Go ahead an' eat," Roland continued to soothe quietly.

As the horse started a cautious nibble, Roland slowly raised his other hand to its nose, touching it very, very lightly. "Good horse. Easy there," he continued to soothe. Roland allowed the horse to finish eating the com while he continued to talk to the horse and to stroke its nose.

Ted stood like a fence post as the horse finished Roland's com and stepped toward him to accept his offering.

"Don't move, Ted," Roland cautioned again, advice hardly needed at the moment.

Roland was now rubbing the horse's neck and was cautiously encircling it with the rope.

He fixed the noose and waited for the horse to finish eating. To the surprise of both boys, he offered no resistance to the rope and tolerated Roland's nearness and touch.

"Ain't he somethin'?" Ted exclaimed as he regained his senses and joined Roland in stroking the neck and head.

"He ain't no wild horse. You sure this is the horse you saw?"

"Yeah, Rolan'. This is the one."

"Look at all these scratches. He musta' been in a fight or somethin'." Roland, holding the rope, petted the horse's shoulder. The horse stood obediently and seemed to relish the attention like a giant puppy.

Ted petted and stroked the neck and head back and forth, beaming a triumphant smile.

"Good horse! Good horse!" he kept repeating. Then he walked to the front and, facing the horse head-on, rubbed the nose with both hands–one on each side–and looked straight into its eyes. It was an electrifying, intimate moment and, for the first time, Ted addressed the horse with the authority of ownership. "Good boy, Spectrum, good boy."

Ted Crockett beamed with pride, standing straight and puffing out his boyish chest.

Roland had worked his way along the side of the horse to the rump. "Boy, look at all these scars and scratches." He examined the rump more closely. "This right here tells the story."

"What, Rolan'?" Ted was busy loving the horse's head.

"This scar looks like… ." Roland squinted his eyes in concentration, running his fingers over a scar that, among the others, distinctly revealed the small letter 'b'. He looked back toward Ted, who was lost in stroking the horse's head. "Ted… ."

"What?" Ted's question was automatic, not conscious enough to interrupt the bond that was developing between him and the horse.

Roland petted his way back toward the head. "Ted, this is a Brotchell horse!"

Some unseen power flipped a switch in Ted. His smile disappeared and his face went blank. "They musta' whipped 'em like crazy," Roland continued. "He prob'bly just ran away."

The shock devastated Ted. A serious frown etched his face and obliterated the joy reflected there just a moment earlier. His hands ceased rubbing and petting the horse and his eyes, wide and large with excitement moments before, now wanted to squeeze out tears. The crash from euphoria to reality strained his voice. "I don't believe it," he squeaked.

"Their brand is on the rump."

Ted felt crushed. "What we gonna' do, Rolan'?"

The horse jerked its head as though sensing the tension. "Steady now," Roland commanded gently, gripping the rope. "Good horse. Hold on, now. Steady, steady."

Ted's words squeezed out like toothpaste out of a tube. "Think I can keep 'em anyway?"

"I dunno."

"He ran away, didn't he? Ted emphasized, regaining a little of his spunk. "He ran away. Don't that make 'em anybody's horse?" The horse became nervous. "Easy there, Spectrum." His words were calming and he petted the nose as the horse stepped backward. Calling him Spectrum already came easily and naturally.

"We better see what Pa thinks. If you plan on keepin' 'em, Pa will have to know every thin '."

Ted felt better, though not too anxious to reveal his adventures to his father. "Le'me take the rope," he implored, reaching out for it. "C'mon, Spectrum," he commanded, tugging lightly on the rope. The horse obeyed.

Roland cautioned: "Better stop callin' 'em that 'til you're sure you can keep 'em."

Ted paid no attention to the warning. "Think I can ride 'em?" Ted began feeling some excitement again.

"Better not," Roland responded "There's no tellin' what he might do if you try to get on 'em. I don't think you better try it. Besides, the Brotchells prob'bly have 'em all spooked up an' scared."

Ted shuddered as he remembered the time he was in their corral. "You think he was in the corral that time…" he flushed with embarrassment, "that time I was in the Brotchell corral?"

"Don'no. He coulda' been. But he coulda' been livin' in the woods a long time, too."

Roland glanced at the horse. "Don't look like he's been taken care of much."

The trio continued toward the pen. Ted's smile returned although it was not as broad as before and it was set on a worried face. When they arrived at the pen, Roland opened the gate and Ted led the horse in.

Once inside, Ted rubbed the horse's neck. "Good boy, Spectrum," he said softly.

"You wait here. I'll be back." Then he slowly, reluctantly, released the rope and let it fall from the horse's neck. "There you go, Spectrum," he assured the horse as he backed slowly away. The horse exercised its freedom by trotting a circle around the pen, stopping abruptly in front of an absorbed Ted.

"Where did that corne from?" Pa Crockett's disapproving voice snapped Ted's concentration like the crash of a thunderbolt, and he stiffened at the sound.

Roland saved the moment. "He was out by the lake, Pa. Ted told me he'd seen 'ern out there a few times ... looks like he was beat up or somethin' ... I think he's a Brotchell horse."

"Why you think that?"

"Looks like their brand on 'em. Look here." He invited his father to study the horse's side and rump.

Anxiety gripped Ted like a vise as he watched his father and brother examine the small 'b' on the horse's rump.

"Lotta' scars and scratches," observed Pa Crockett.

"He prob'bly ran away."

"I think you're about right."

Ted knew his father was wise in the way of horses, having owned and worked them on the land most of his life. He respected his father's sternness and he pressed back against the fence railing, tense as the fate of his horse was being decided. He waited anxiously for his father to pronounce sentence, one that he feared.

Pa Crockett inhaled deeply and began walking out of the pen. "We have enough trouble from them boneheads already," he ruled. "I don't want 'em comin' aroun' here givin' us more."

"Pa," Ted interjected bravely, "since they beat 'em up an' he ran away...don't that make 'em anybody's horse?" His voice trailed off weakly into a slight tremble as he suddenly realized some flaw in his statement.

"He's still their horse. How'd you boys catch 'em, anyway?"

Ted's heart skipped at least one beat and Roland continued as spokesman.

"We just walked up to 'em, Pa," he lied. "He didn't run or anythin'."

Pa Crockett chuckled as he glanced at the rope draped over the gate. "I suppose you boys always walk around the lake with a rope in your hands." He chuckled again at the mischief of his boys. Roland's face flushed from the shame of trying to fool his father.

Ted felt relief that his father took it lightly and he pressed the good fortune. "Think we can keep 'em, Pa?"

Pa Crockett, returning to serious silence, began to walk toward the house. The boys followed, glancing at each other for support.

Ted took advantage of his father's hesitation. "The Brotchells never come aroun' here...they'd never see 'em here... ."

"Nah!" Pa Crockett interrupted. "Don't want any more trouble outta' them idiots," he ruled again.

Ted knew that his father was serious when he began substituting words for the Brotchell's name. The trio walked a little farther before Pa Crockett pronounced sentence.

"After breakfast, you boys take 'em back out to where you found 'em. He'll most likely hang aroun' out there, but I don't want 'em here."

Ted felt like his heart plunged into a deep hole and a cloud of depression began forming over him. He wanted to plead, but didn't dare. Once Pa Crockett made his decision, he seldom changed it. In fact, his temper would most likely explode if Ted pressed for a change.

"I'm not hungry," Ted muttered suddenly as he turned around to go back to the pen.

Once there, he pressed against the gate, planted his elbows on the top rail and dropped his chin into his hands. Fixing his eyes on the horse, he felt a familiar anger return–an anger of consuming hatred for the Brotchells. The hatred evoked frustration, and frustration induced tears which quickly turned into private, painful, uninhibited sobbing.

He was still hanging on the gate when Roland returned. There followed a time of no conversation, but communication certainly took place as Roland consoled his brother.

The atmosphere was that of a wake, as if someone had died–it was almost solemn. Soon, reluctantly and still in silence, the boys led the horse back to the lake where Ted made sure that he was turned loose in front of a small pile of corn.

As Roland started to return to the house, Ted finally spoke. "I wanna' stay here a while." He hardly heard Roland's O.K. as he welded his attention on the horse, petting and rubbing. Somewhere between its nose and neck, Ted, in the anguish of rejection, lost his sense of reality. "I'll get you. You're gonna' be mine," he promised the horse. "I'll find some way to get you." As he looked the horse in the face, Ted Crockett sealed his promise with a teardrop.

7

An Unbelievable Vision

In November, Nature took out paints and brushes and transformed the countryside into pictures of autumn. Texas at the Crockett homestead offered nature a moderate pallet: tallows, sumacs and maples mingled with evergreens. Other trees, like the mesquite and oak, didn't contribute much color, but they did add texture to the landscape.

Over this artistry, migratory birds flapped and glided in truncated V's, in bunches and in long, strung out ropes. Ted, visiting the horse by the lake, watched a small flock of ducks circle and glide to a landing, settling on the water after a short skid on its surface.

Ted liked this season second only to spring. The changes always stirred a creativity and an energy he frequently did not understand how to direct–or, toward what. But today, he suffered a totally new conflict, an emotion with which he had never had to wrestle the way he did now. Since releasing the horse–as directed by his father–he continued to visit him and secretly brought him corn. The two had become friends over the past two weeks and Ted had even taken to riding him, with the horse's complete consent and cooperation.

This morning, after the horse muzzled corn from his hand, Ted grabbed a handful of mane and swung himself onto the bare back. Sitting proudly, he commanded, "let's go, Spectrum," as his knees gave the horse's ribs a gentle squeeze. Already the understanding between boy and horse was such that the horse responded immediately. Sitting on the horse's back, Ted experienced great pleasure and he allowed the horse to walk around the clearing until, without plan or design, he guided the horse to Main Trail and into the woods.

"Easy there, boy," he ordered as branches and twigs brushed against his legs. Arriving at a small clearing in the path, Ted circled the horse around and reversed the trek. Suddenly, he heard a shout, not too far away. "Whoa, Spectrum," he whispered, pulling back on the mane. The horse obeyed and the two became like a statue in the woods as Ted listened for more human sounds. There! He heard it again! He shifted toward the direction of the sound but the underbrush prevented him from seeing very far, and the woods made the exact direction of the sounds too vague. He could make out two, maybe three, different voices, shouting and jabbering. The Brotchells! Must be the Brotchells! The thought chilled Ted's body. Hesitating no longer, he gave the horse a restrained kick to its side. "Let's get outa' here, Spectrum," he ordered. Fear swept over him and he began to breathe heavily. His hands became damp and his face tightened. He looked back, but saw no one. He only heard voices.

"C'mon boy, let's go!" he urged, although a fearful whimper colored his voice.

Because the trail was narrow and winding at this point, he resisted an overwhelming urge to kick the horse into a gallop, an urge re-enforced by fear. As he continued along Main Trail, the voices faded with the distance until, at the lake, he could hear them no more. But he felt weak and his body shook from the scare of one more close encounter with the Brotchells.

Ted guided his horse to the edge of the lake and slid off its back, giving it several grateful pats on the neck. "Good boy, Spectrum." The lake beckoned him and he sat down so close to the water's edge that the toes of his shoes touched the waterline. Drawing up his knees, he hugged his legs and rested his chin. The secure feeling of this favored position melted his fear. He stared into the water, seriously. Not even the ducks on the lake interested him now. Neither did others flying overhead although he inattentively watched their reflection deep in the water collide with the bank and disappear beneath it.

The horse stepped up to the water to drink and Ted shifted his attention to him. He did not want the Brotchells to have him back but he did not know how to prevent it if they were looking for him. For now, he could only continue to sneak corn to feed him. His father must never find out. He thought that maybe the food and friendship would keep the horse around the lake area and keep him from wandering back toward the Brotchell homestead. They would not find him here since they never ventured into this area of the Crockett homestead. He felt sure that the horse would be safe at the lake.

As Ted pondered these things, the serenity around the lake suddenly erupted with the pulse of life: the whirring sound of ducks taking flight, quacking frightfully; the buzz of a flock of blackbirds as they, together as one, turned abruptly and sharply this way and that, again and again. In the commotion, a hawk repeatedly pierced the blackbird flock until, high overhead, it emerged from the milling cloud with a black speck in its talons and flew off with its prize. The flock continued to dodge an imaginary foe until finally it also flew off into the distance. With the danger gone, the ducks returned from their evading flight and made happy and noisy landings on the lake.

Eventually, peace returned to the area and Ted returned to staring into the water. He searched deep among the clouds reflected there for the answer to his problem. In the depth of the scene, a small 'V' of geese appeared. "Maybe they have an answer," he thought as he watched them honk their way across the clouds reflected deep in the lake. But they collided with the bank and slipped underneath it, giving him no answer.

A whinny from the horse shook Ted out of his thoughts and he turned around to see the horse standing alert, ears up and head high, staring toward the woods. Ted felt a flash of fear - the Brotchells had followed him! Instinct urged him to mount the horse and gallop to the house. He bounced up from his position, got the horse and was about to swing himself onto its back when a whinny from the edge of the woods froze him in place. Turning his eyes in that direction, he beheld a shiny, black horse at the edge of the clearing. In open mouth disbelief and total surprise, he looked back and forth several times from the black horse to his horse as a symphony began: a whinny from one horse answered by the other, back and forth. Abruptly, before Ted recovered enough to do anything, the stately newcomer turned gracefully and sprinted into the woods.

Ted stood breathless and astounded, staring in the direction of the vanished horse.

Fading hoofbeats reminded him of his first encounter with hoofbeats in the late evening two months ago. Puzzled, he turned slowly toward his horse. "You're...you're not...the one I saw," he said slowly, breathing the words quietly. After more puzzling thought, he emphasized loudly, "You're the wrong horse!" The confusion brought to his eyes a glisten that reflected the emotion in his heart. "There really is a wild horse out there," he informed his animal. His face began to loosen, his eyes grew wide, his mouth opened and the beginning of a grin appeared, growing into a broad smile as he repeated jubilantly:

"There really is!" Taking a deep breath, he shouted: "There really is!"

It took a while for Ted to recover from the stunning shock of this new discovery, but he felt the same tingling excitement he had felt that late evening in October. His eyes focused on the spot where the wild horse had stood just moments before. His excitement built until it burst into a huge thrill. Again taking a deep breath, he breathed a long, gleeful and gushing "WOW!"

Unable to hold all this within himself, he left the horse and raced around the lake toward the house to announce the news. Finding Roland at the woodpile, he called, "Rolan'". Almost out of breath, he called again: "Rolan', there really is a wild horse out there!" He tried to catch his breath. "I seen 'em," he called as he caught up to his brother, "a real, wild one, Rolan'! I was there with Spectrum…an' this wild, black horse comes out of the woods…an' he was so shiny…and' he an' Spectrum whinnied at each other…an'…"

Roland held up a hand. "C'mon, Ted," he said impatiently. "C'mon, leave it alone. We already caught one wild horse."

"Rolan'," Ted gushed on in his excitement, "we didn't catch the wild one! I seen the real wild one! I really seen 'em, Rolan'!" Ted was ready for tears of frustration. "I was there with Spectrum and the wild horse came out of the woods an'…Rolan', you gotta' believe me!"

His brother said nothing as he arranged a log into position, raised his axe over his head and swung it down forcefully at the log to the resounding crack of splitting wood. Reaching down to rearrange the remains, he said: "Even if there is one, Ted, you need to just forget about 'em. You make it sound like the woods are full of wild horses runnin' aroun' like rabbits or somethin'." He smiled faintly, but got serious with the log again.

"But I seen 'em, Rolan'! ... I seen 'em!".

"Well, maybe so, but forget about tryin' to catch 'em. The one we caught was a scared Brotchell animal…if he'd really been wild, we woulda' never got close to 'em. Or worse, he coulda' turned on us."

Ted sat down on the partial remains of a tree trunk, safely away from Roland's axe, and pondered a moment. Getting up, he picked up an axe and whacked out his frustration on a helpless log. Roland stepped back to avoid the chips of wood that the log shot out as if in self-defense. Finally, Ted exhausted his energy and frustration and sat down again, emotionally deflated like a balloon that had lost its air.

Roland sat down on a nearby log. "Ted, why do you work yourself up like this every time you want somethin', or every time you think you see somethin' you want?" He removed his cap. "Sure, its O.K. to want stuff, but some stuff is just past your reach."

"Rolan'…" Ted looked momentarily at a flock of ducks overhead. "Rolan'…," he paused again. "You think…you think there's a way to catch the wild horse?"

"You don't give up, but you're not goin' to get me into another stunt like that. You know, we were kinda' dumb catchin' the Brotchell horse." Roland picked up a long sliver of wood and sent it spinning through the air like a propeller.

"But we could… ."

Roland interrupted. "It was dumb, Ted! Dumb! Dumb! Dumb! Why, if he'd been wild, we coulda' got hoofed or kicked…a wild stallion isn't just goin' to stand there an' let you put a rope on his neck."

Roland's remarks brought back a brief memory of the trampling Ted suffered in the Brotchell corral. "Still, would be somethin'…, to try to catch 'em," he fancied.

Roland released the hold on his patience. "You just don't give up, do you?" he spouted as he got up to leave. "Get off it! Find somethin' else to do!" With a frustrating gesture, he departed, muttering disbelief.

Ted continued to sit and brood as he kicked at the wood chips littering the ground. The honking of geese suddenly erupted as a flock disorganized and frantically pumped their wings, trying to gain the safety of altitude. Just as Ted looked up, he heard a distant gun blast. Prob'bly the Brotchells, he thought. Uninterested, he returned his attention to the wood chips, scooting them into a little hill with his foot. Then he gave the hill a kick that sent the chips flying.

The sadness, gloom and frustration Ted felt reflected the loss of direction he sometimes suffered when faced with a problem, and at those times he would do foolish things. Roland was the only person with whom he felt confident, and now he felt let down by him too.

Sometimes, he would approach his Ma and Pa about such matters, but he always felt uneasy doing so. His parents always seemed distant to his problems, always seemed to assume that everything was fine; or they simply did not believe Ted and corrected or scolded him. His father, especially, seemed at times stern and disinterested. Maybe he just misunderstood or Ted did not know how to express himself. He respected and loved his parents, but he wished they would listen.

Ted thought about these things and was about to drown in self-pity when he saw his father returning in the old car, bringing fresh meat from the meat club. The meat club had become a Saturday morning ritual where members of the club from miles around–except the Brotchells who refused to associate with their neighbors–would gather at the home of one of the members to divide up a carcass of beef. One member kept a record of the amount and cut each received so that, over a period of time, each family received all parts of a carcass: ribs one time, rump the next, neck another, and so on. The club had fourteen member families, all agreeing to abide by the rotation process.

Each also agreed, in turn, to provide a steer for the slaughter.

The process put fresh meat on fourteen tables at least once a week, and these Saturdays were always days of delicious dining. Ted enjoyed the fresh steak or stew or chili with the added joy of fresh bread and pastries that Ma Crockett baked in abundance to accompany the feast. He always looked forward to these suppertimes and he always ate what appeared to be a week's portion.

Pa Crockett's arrival dissolved some of Ted's self-pity as he began to imagine the supper table. He got up and hurried to meet his father to check the portion of meat for the week. He might even be asked to help in cutting it up.

Pa Crockett was talking to Ma Crockett as he approached. "That darn Sutterly cheated again," he grumbled as he lifted the bloody sack containing the meat out of the car. "We should vote on not meeting at Sutterly's house any more. Seems like we always meet there." Pa Crockett continued to complain on the way into the house. "I know he always helps himself to a steak supper on Friday after the carcass is hung up in his meat house." Pa Crockett clinched his jaws. "You can always see where he cut off a piece." A reddening face and bulging blood vessels on his neck forecast Pa Crockett's outburst. "He always cheats!" he roared as he slammed the door behind him.

Because of the possibility that there may be harsh language or arguments, Ted was never allowed to accompany his father to any of these club meetings. So he always pictured the event as men standing around the beef carcass like vultures waiting their turn while Sutterly helped himself like a lion after a fresh kill.

"Be thankful we got a portion," Ma Crockett said.

"Sure, look what we got!" Pa Crockett bellowed as he slammed the sack on the kitchen table. "Same as last week!"

Ma Crockett opened the sack to find a portion of neck as Pa Crockett thundered: "That damn Sutterly cheated on the book, too. He got us down for a foreleg last Saturday. I know damn well we got a neck." At that, Pa Crockett stormed out of the house.

Somewhere around the Crockett homestead, some creature or some structure would be so unfortunate as to receive the brunt of Pa Crockett's anger.

Ted did not like being around when his father was in this kind of rage. It frightened him and he stole quietly out the door and made his way toward the chicken coop. He considered this to be a good time to do his unpleasant weekly chore of scooping out the droppings and taking them in a wheelbarrow to the field. Every Saturday, he tried to delay this chore as long as he could. Today, under the cloud of his father's storm, he took the opportunity to be busy.

That afternoon, Ted sat on a stool by the barn watching bunches of blackbirds circle overhead, alight in the field, only to fly up again and repeat the process. His mind, however, wrestled with thoughts of the wild horse.

Pa Crockett approached across the yard. "What you doin', Ted?"

Ted quickly checked his mind to see if he was supposed to be doing some chore, for he didn't know if his father was still in a rage from the morning. Satisfied that all his Saturday jobs were finished, he replied with a relaxed: "Nothin', Pa ... just thinkin'."

His father chuckled knowingly. "About a horse?"

Ted blushed at the truth, grateful for his father's softened mood, and said meekly:

"Yeah, Pa." His father sat down on the step in front of the barn door. After a few moments, Ted asked: "Pa, you think..." he summoned up all his courage, "you think I could keep the Brotchell horse...he just stays out by the lake and it don't look like the Brotchells want 'em an'..."

His father interrupted: "That's already been settled."

His father's reply had the stamp of a finality that frightened Ted and he shrank into himself, regretting that he had even brought up the subject. He wisely decided to make no mention of the new sighting of the wild horse.

A shell of silence encrusted father and son until Pa Crockett's voice cracked it.

"Wanna' shoot some geese?"

Ted brightened but replied uncertainly. "Yeah, Pa."

"Maybe the three of us can go out this evenin' an' really bring back some meat."

"Sure, Pa. I'd like that." Ted felt better that his father had mellowed since the morning and he suspected that the 'neck of beef' probably was the motive for the goose hunt.

"I'll go out an' take a look at the blind."

"Good idea, Ted."

As Ted started to rise, a special feeling crept over him and held him fast - that feeling of a special connection with his father that prompted love, gratitude and appreciation. He spoke before he meant to. "Pa, remember when you got shot?"

"Remember?" his father growled. "I still got a scar that's not healed all the way." Ted suddenly realized that he'd asked a dumb question, but he was glad he had brought up the subject. "Pa, them bucks that were fightin' in the clearing when you got shot..." Ted paused to gather courage as he suddenly turned to face his father. "I seen 'em, Pa, an' I heard the shots...an' I heard them Brotchells... ."

Pa Crockett appeared unmoved. "Where were you?"

Ted found it difficult to determine if his father was surprised, glad or what; he knew for sure when he was mad. "In the woods at the edge of the clearin', at

Main Trail. I just happened to be there, Pa, an' I was watchin' them bucks fight…I didn't know you was there too."

"That's O.K. Ted. I stayed pretty quiet. Guess you did too."

"We musta' been close, Pa, cause the shots came from my right an' you musta' been directly across the clearing from them Brotchells."

"If I knew you was there, I woulda' hollered."

There was a long pause before Pa Crockett muttered: "Them Brotchells are worse than Sutterly."

"Sorry I didn't help, Pa," Ted apologized.

"That's alright, Ted. I know you woulda' if you knew I was there."

Ted felt his father's tenderness during that rare moment, just like when he gave Ted the old plow horse on his birthday. Silence again engulfed father and son as they sat hunched over, elbows on knees, heads bent downward as though studying the ground. Finally, Ted got up.

"I'll go take a look at the blind." He felt a relief, a lightness, the heavy weight of his secret finally lifted. The fresh feeling put a bounce into his step, and he walked briskly toward the hunting blind in the field, humming one of the many tunes that always seemed to be in his head.

After inspecting the blind–only the hay needed an adjustment here and there - he sat down on the ground inside it, reached into his pocket and pulled out his harmonica. Closing his eyes and taking a deep breath, Ted Crockett played out feelings embedded in his soul, emotions wrapped up in his being, the touch of eternity that stirred his heart. At that moment, Ted Crockett felt peace.

8

The Dream Reappears

December felt crisp. It was the first Saturday of the month and, as the eastern sky was just beginning to light the world, two bundled up figures arrived at the blind. The sounds of geese were already in the air as Ted and Roland hurried to set out newspaper decoys. They then settled down inside the blind, insuring that the shotguns were loaded and ready. It didn't take long for the birds to appear.

"Here comes a bunch," Ted whispered as though the geese could hear him. "Be real still."

Anticipation mounted in the blind. The honking of the geese changed to a constant ruckus as the ones in the air tried to communicate with the decoys on the ground. Wings stretched out in a glide, the geese flew almost directly over the blind where the suspense exploded in two gun shots. Instantly, the geese honked alarm and peddled their wings to escape the danger, but one dropped out of the bunch and fell to earth like a feathery stone.

"Hey, we got one," Ted shouted joyously as he bolted out of the blind to get the prize. "Hurry up, Ted. There's more comin'."

Once again, expectancy mounted in the blind only to subside as the geese drifted to one side, out of range for a shot. Others flew around, some far, some near, but not near enough. Their honking, however, filled the crisp morning air like a surround symphony.

"Who you think got 'em?" Ted wondered as the boys were returning to the house.

"Don't matter none. I just figgered there would be more of 'em come our way." "Yeah," Ted agreed.

The boys walked in silence for a while until Ted spoke.

"Rolan', I been worryin' about somethin'."

"What?"

"Well, you know I been sorta' visitin' the horse out at the lake... ."

"Sorta' visitin?" Roland chuckled. "Heck, you been livin' out there."

"Well, the past coupla' days, he ain't been there."

"Prob'bly just found a better place or somethin'."

"You think them Brotchells got 'em?"

"No tellin' what they got. I try not to think about 'em."

Ted's voice sank a little. "Anyway, I miss that horse."

"Funny you called 'em 'that horse'. What happened to Spectrum?"

"Oh, I call 'em Spectrum. I think he's learned his name already." Ted's voice brightened, then fell. "I sure miss 'em."

"You goin' out there this mornin'?"

"Yeah, right after we clean the goose."

At the house, under the cedar trees, stood a weathered table which, over the years, had seen on its grooved surface chickens being plucked and cleaned, machinery being repaired, vegetables being cut and rabbits being dressed. On it the boys put the lifeless form of the goose. Roland began pulling the soft, light down off the breast, depositing handfuls of the fluffy tufts into a paper bag - the makings of a future pillow or featherbed. Meanwhile, Ted whistled off into the house and returned with a pail of boiling water for the scalding of the bird. Before submerging it, Roland cut off the wing tips which, after drying out, would become dusters and whiskbrooms.

Ted never really enjoyed the gutting of anything, but had learned to endure the ritual.

Cleaning this bird was particularly unpleasant since one of the pellets had hit the intestines and made quite a mess. Nevertheless, the chore was accomplished and Roland took the dressed goose into the house where Ma Crockett would turn it into a feast. Meanwhile, Ted delivered the bucket of entrails to the pasture where chickens fought over them.

Leaving the bucket to be picked up on his return, Ted eagerly hurried to the lake, expecting Spectrum to be standing there waiting for him. His eyes searched the entire clearing but it was as empty as his heart. He sat down on a log and stared at the woods as though the horse was about to come out. The longer he waited, the deeper became the empty feeling. Once again, needing the support of his music, he reached into his pocket and drew out his harmonica. Closing his eyes, he played another slow, drawn-out melody.

As the last trailing note faded away, Ted opened his eyes and looked around. There was no one there. No one cared. The ducks on the lake were minding their own affairs; the geese overhead were honking their own destiny; the creatures in the woods did not even come out to hear his music. Even the horse did not come. He felt alone.

Getting up, he re-pocketed the harmonica and began a slow, depressing stroll along the lake shore. Crawfish slipped into their holes or rocketed back into the water and minnows scattered to greater depths as he approached. All appeared reluctant to face him in such a mood. His spirit felt empty like the trees that the winter had stripped bare. Sullen, he stopped and looked over the clearing around the lake one more time before returning to the house.

By mid-December, Ted worried long hours about the fate of his horse. Leaning against the gate of the pen, he clasped the top rail and, resting his chin on his hands, sank into thought, staring blankly into the pen.

"What you watchin'?" Pa Crockett's voice shattered the silence.

"Oh, nothin', Pa," Ted stammered. "Just thinkin'."

Pa Crockett's belly jiggled with one of his understanding chuckles. "In your head, you was on the back of that horse, racin' aroun' the lake or somewhere." His mouth broke into a grin and his raised eyebrows questioned: "Huh?"

Ted never understood how his father always knew what he was thinking. "Yeah, Pa. Guess so."

"Why ain't you out behind the lake, sneakin' corn to that Brotchell horse?"

Ted flushed with embarrassment. His father knew everything. His sneaking corn out of the barn had not been so sneaky after all. He avoided turning his red face toward his father as Pa Crockett bellied up to the fence along Ted's side, smiling one of his on/off smiles that suggested mischief.

Ted shifted his position. "Pa, I ain't seen that horse for a coupla' weeks now. He don't come aroun' no more."

"That's prob'bly best"

"What do you think happened to 'em, Pa?'

"Aw, you never know about horses, Ted, especially one that's free to roam. He mighta' just got the roamin' spirit an' is out there somewhere happy as can be." Pa Crockett rubbed his chin thoughtfully, "Or somethin' coulda' happened to 'em...he mighta' got sick...an' died."

"NO!" Ted shot the word forcefully at this father.

"But that's prob'bly not so," Pa Crockett consoled Ted as he backed away from the gate and began to leave. "Don't worry your head about it."

Ted remained glued to the gate. He did not want to dwell on such a tragedy happening to Spectrum, but the thought disturbed his mind; it drilled into his heart; it wrung out his stomach. Suddenly, Ted did not feel well physically or emotionally. Letting go of the gate, he hastened around the pen, past the chicken coop, skirted the woodpile and ran the rest of the way to the lake, ignoring the ducks that quacked a greeting at him.

Reaching the opening of Main Trail, he entered the woods and began searching the familiar trails and clearings. Although he had walked these trials many times before, a new fear gripped him at each turn and released only when he did not find a horse, dead or alive.

Eventually, his search brought him to Big Swale, the stage of nothing but tragedy: the bucks fighting; his father being shot; the wild horse being mistreated by the Brotchells. Continuing his search, he entered the clearing of Big Swale and was about half the way across when a shout startled him.

"Hey, Crockett, what you doin' out there?"

A terrible fear seized Ted, a fear like the one he had experienced in the Brotchell corral. He turned toward the area of the woods from which the voice had come.

"Better git outa' there." The voice commanded, "unless you wanna' become a trophy."

Ted suddenly realized that he had walked into the Brotchell line of fire. They were waiting for deer to come into the clearing. In near panic, he dashed back to the safety of the woods, to the safety of Main Trail. Behind him, he heard guffaws and laughter. He ran a safe distance down Main Trail before he slowed down, making sure that the Brotchells were not following, and hurried on. He was terrified, angry, frustrated…just plain mad.

By the time he arrived at the lake, anger so gripped him that he picked up clods of dirt and, in a rage, threw them at the ducks that were peacefully floating on the water. He hurled one at any bird unfortunate enough to fly by. As a final outburst of frustration, he affixed a clay ball to the end of a stick and ferociously lobbed it at a small bunch of blackbirds.

Finally, his rage spent, Ted sat down on the bank in the familiar chin-on-knees posture and fixed a brooding stare into the water. Where he should have seen a fish, he saw a horse. Instead of seeing leaves floating on the water, he saw Brotchells running around. Where calm and peace should have come out of the lake to heal, he saw dangerous whirlpools swirling. Picking up small clods of dirt, he attacked and bombed the floating leaves, angry that they would not sink.

Suddenly getting up, he stomped along the edge of the lake in the direction of the house. A duck on the lake spoke to him in a series of long quacks. "Aw, shut up!" Ted spit out as he picked up a clod of dirt and threw it at the duck, which quacked in protest and flew off.

He arrived at the house in this bitter frame of mind. He entered and slammed the door behind him. From somewhere that seemed far away, his mother's voice pierced the gloom. "Ted, you know better than that. Go back an' shut the door like you're supposed to."

Ted retraced his steps grudgingly, opened the door and performed a controlled close. "Now, you just watch that temper," Ma Crockett advised.

He arrived in his room subdued only a little by the door slamming incident. Flopping down on his bed, he settled in to brood.

The next morning, Sunday, after church–he didn't remember anything about the sermon, but he did remember exchanging smiles with Wanda–Ted was still mad at the Brotchells, although his anger had tempered. At the woodpile, he assembled pieces of boards, intent on building a trap to catch small animals. Hammering the boards in the framework of a box, he attached chicken wire to all four sides and finished the top with wooden planks. Sitting down on a log, he fashioned thin pieces of wood into a figure '4', which would be the trigger that tripped the snare. He tied a small head of grain from the haystack onto the trigger, and the trap was complete. In the evening, he would set it out in the pasture where he had seen evidence of rabbits.

From the woodpile, it was natural for Ted to go to the lake. The harmonica came out of his pocket and he played his way to the far side. Suddenly, he stopped his tune and bent down to study the ground. Looking toward the woods, he whispered excitedly to himself: "Spectrum was here!" Maybe it was not Spectrum, but a horse–some horse–had been on this very spot…probably this very morning.

Instinctively, he hurried toward Main Trail, scanning the area in anticipation. Tense excitement shivered his body as he entered the woods and, walking quickly, he peered into every opening in the brush until once again he arrived at Big Swale. But fear of encountering the Brotchells again held him back and he only scanned the clearing from the safety of the brush. He imagined his horse coming out of the woods, proud and majestic. Engrossed in his imagery, he did not notice the movement at the southern edge of the clearing. So when the horse did emerge, imagery melted into reality and the result seized Ted in a spine-tingling, goose bump elation. Seeing what he wanted to see, he was eager for a reunion.

Bursting out of his hiding place, Ted ran toward the animal, shouting "Spectrum!" As the startled horse bolted and disappeared into the woods, Ted suddenly realized that, for the second time, he actually saw the wild horse that had galloped into his life that late evening in October. Totally surprised and completely amazed, Ted bubbled with joy. He felt a vengeful satisfaction and fulfilling excitement as he stared into the woods where the horse had vanished.

"I seen 'em again...the wild one!" he said out loud in a restrained voice. "I knew it! I knew it!" he repeated triumphantly as he ran to the spot where the horse had entered the woods. "I knew I seen 'em before," he said as he reached the edge of the woods. He entered and followed a trail for a short distance before he realized he would never catch up to the startled animal. Retracing his steps, he emerged from the woods and stopped on the very spot where the wild horse had stood just moments before. Observing the hoof prints on the ground, he exclaimed emphatically: "He was here! He was right here!"

The clearing now became too small to contain the exuberance of the boy of twelve.

Looking around, Ted repeated forcefully: "He was right here!" The satisfaction of knowing that he had been right all along brought a swell of pride. "I knew I seen 'em!" he said again out loud. "I knew all along there was a wild horse!" Out of shear joy, he started walking around in a circle, repeating out loud: "He was here! He was here!" Eager to tell someone, he dashed across the clearing and along Main Trail as fast as its curves and bushes allowed. But, by the time he reached the lake, much of his excitement was spent as he concluded that no one would believe him, just as before. He stopped at the bank of the lake and sat down to study the water, hoping to find in it the answer to how he could prove the existence of the wild horse. "There's gotta' be a way," he muttered to the lake. Resting his chin on his knees, he re-lived the scene that played out on the stage of Big Swale just a short while ago.

9

Reality Sinks In

Later that afternoon, when the Bereneks came to visit, Ted got right to the point with Roland and Chris as soon as Chris got out of the car. "I have somethin' to show you in Big Swale."

"What's there?" Chris asked.

"C'mon, lem'me show you."

Roland interrupted. "Ted, you're not goin' to show us another horse, are you?" Ted looked at Wanda who stood by the car as though waiting for Ted to invite her along. In his enthusiasm, he had not even greeted her. He felt pulled in her direction, but also saw a chance to prove that the wild horse really existed. So he turned his attention back to Roland and Chris and announced firmly: "I wa'na show you where I saw the wild horse about noon today."

Chris exclaimed: "Hey! That sounds excitin'. Let's go!"

"No!" Roland stated. That ain't excitin'. Ted has been seein' this wild horse for a coupla' months now an' all we got out of it was catchin' a Brotchell horse. Now he thinks there's another one out there."

Ted stomped his foot for emphasis. "There is!"

Roland got a little terse. "Ted, get off it. You prob'bly saw another Brotchell horse, if you saw one at all."

"I saw 'em! Doggone, he's real!"

"C'mon, Chris," Roland invited, "let's go shoot some blackbirds."

Watching the boys leave, Ted could not control his frustration and he fought back tears.

From behind him came a voice: "I'll go look."

Ted had forgotten about Wanda and did not notice her approach. At the sound of her voice, he tried to hide tearful eyes. "You ain't suppose to see me cry," he sniffed.

"That's O.K. I cry sometimes."

"Yeah, but you're a girl."

"So what?"

"Well '" it's O.K. for girls to cry."

"I can still go look at your wild horse…or, where he was."

"Naw," Ted said, drying his eyes, "I cain't take you into the woods."

"Why not?"

"Well '" you're a girl."

"So what?"

"My Ma an' Pa would not like that an' they'd prob'ly punish me or somethin'." He looked at her with a little longing. "But I'd like to take you there, to Big Swale."

"That would be fun. I never been there." Wanda bounced in anticipation.

"But I cain't take you."

"Yeah,…'cause I'm a girl," she muttered, lowering her eyes.

Long minutes of silence followed as Ted and Wanda meandered toward the barn…aimlessly…for no reason. Finally Wanda spoke. "What was the Brotchell horse Roland mentioned?"

"'Aw, him an' me caught this horse out by the lake…I'd seen 'em before…an' we caught 'em an' it turned out that he was a Brotchell horse…prob'bly ran away 'cause he had scratches an' marks on his side an' back where they beat 'em."

"How'd you know it was a Brotchell horse?"

"He had this little "b" on his rump. Pa wouldn't let me keep 'em, though. I had to let the horse go. But he stayed aroun' the lake and I fed 'em an' even rode 'em. But now he's gone...don't know where he is...I really miss 'em."

"Why don't you just forget 'em...since he's gone?"

Ted turned to face her. "Wanda," he said seriously, "I want my own horse real bad. Been dreamin' about 'em an' thinkin' about 'em. I really want one."

"For a while, you had that one your Pa gave you."

Ted felt embarrassed. "Yeah" he said, almost inaudibly.

The conversation bantered on and off for some time but, because of Ted's sullen mood, they mostly just sat and talked little through the afternoon until they were called to supper. Afterwards, the Bereneks went home and Ted went to his room to brood some more.

For the next few days, he appeared lost in thought and wandered around as though he had lost his best friend. He felt alone, frustrated and empty, feelings brought on by his not being able to prove that the wild horse was real.

'Ted's already thinkin' about Christmas' he heard Ma Crockett tell his father. The truth only made him lonelier.

As the month progressed, Ted's mood mellowed, partly due to the coming Christmas season. But the horse and things of the woods were never out of his mind.

One evening, lying on their bed, Ted and Roland stared out the window, watching car headlights coming down the dirt road that bordered the Crockett homestead. The lights slowed down at the wooded area of the pasture. Suddenly they stopped. Blam! Blam! Two gunshots shattered the evening.

"That's prob'bly them Brotchells shootin' rabbits again," Roland guessed.

"Yeah. But them's our rabbits," Ted stated as though the Brotchells were stealing their food.

"They're close to where I set the trap." A moment of silence passed. "Wish we could go chase 'em off."

"I don't wanna' face 'em...especially at night when they got guns."

The boys watched as men with flashlights walked around the pasture. Then all flashlights went back to the headlights and they departed. Once again, the silence of the evening settled over the homestead.

"Maybe we can put some wooden rabbits out there an' make them Brotchells feel stupid when they shoot 'em."

"Yeah," Ted agreed, mischief reflecting on his face. "Them Brotchells been comin' aroun' almost every week. We can have the wooden rabbit ready for 'em next time."

The following morning, in the workshop, the boys busily cut rabbit profiles out of pieces of boards. "Hold this while I drill the eye." Ted then pressed a marble into the hole to give the decoy a reflecting eye for more realism in the dim searchlight of the hunters. They made three decoys in this manner and, attaching small stakes to each one, took them to the pasture and set them out–one here, one there and one over there. They made sure that the decoys were in profile to the hunters' searchlight.

This game took Ted's attention off the horse, but only for a while. With the decoys in place, the horse trotted back into his mind. "Wanna' go with me to the lake?" He wanted very much to share his fmd in Big Swale with Roland, but feared rejection as before. He had to wait for the right moment.

"What we gonna' do there?"

"Oh, we could fool aroun'...maybe sling mud or somethin'."

"Well, guess so."

On the way, Roland asked: "Ever see that horse again?"

Ted's heart stopped. "Nooooo," he lied. "But there's still one out there." He felt uncertain about this being the right time to tell Roland.

"Yeah," Roland smiled.

Ted didn't want the conversation to die. Approaching the lake, he picked up a barrel stave and sent it across the water in a burst of speed. The sudden action brought protests from some ducks as they launched and quacked their way into the sky.

Ted tried to act calm. "I saw some tracks and other stuff out there the other day." He pointed toward the far side of the lake.

"Oh, yeah?"

Ted sent another stave racing across the water. "Yeah. An' I sorta' went into the woods to look aroun'... ." His heart began to pound.

"Find anythin'?"

"Well, sorta'."

"Sorta' what?"

The churning excitement almost turned Ted inside out, but he tried to remain calm.

"Out in the clearing on Main Trail... ."

"Yeah? What?"

"In Big Swale...there was a horse... ."

Trying to remain calm, Ted picked up a clod of dirt and lobbed it into the water. The 'sploosh' was the only response he heard. Roland remained quiet as he, also, lobbed a clod into the lake, almost hitting the same spot as Ted. Ted followed, trying to hit the same spot where Roland had thrown. Spontaneously, a contest ensued with one trying to hit the 'bullseye' the other made on the water. The frenzy released some tension, and Ted relaxed. Feeling he had Roland's confidence, he continued his quest.

"Wanna' go take a look?"

"At what?"

"At Big Swale, to see if there's anythin' there."

"Nah!"

Ted struggled to control himself He tried not to pressure Roland.

"Maybe...we could just...ah, kinda' wander through the woods... ."

Roland smiled. "I don't really feel like that. You're tryin' to get me into somethin' stupid again. Think I'll go finish fixin' the chicken coop before Ma or Pa get after me."

Ted felt the opportunity slipping away like a bar of wet soap in a hot bathtub. He tried to suppress his disappointment, frustration and even anger. With a blush starting to appear on his face and tension knotting his throat, he blurted out: "Rolan', I seen the wild horse in the clearing! I seen 'em!" His eyes opened wide with excitement. "I spooked 'em, an' he ran off into the woods and...I couldn't find 'em...but he was there! He was black an' powerful!"

Roland studied his brother. "You really believe that, don't you?"

"You bet I do, Rolan', 'cause it really happened. He really was there. I seen 'em!" Ted inhaled a fluttering sniff.

Without a word, Roland began walking toward Main Trail. Surprised, Ted quickly followed his brother into the woods. Approaching Big Swale, the boys slowed their step and quietly approached the clearing. Just as they were about to reach the edge of the woods, two gunshots shattered the silence. The boys froze in terror. Now they heard voices.

"Ho-hooooo!" shouted one.

"Got 'em," yelled another.

Familiar voices! "The Brotchells!" Ted whispered. "Them...Brotchells!"

Roland suddenly whispered a realization "we're lucky we weren't in the line of fire.

We coulda' been shot...like Pa." His voice quivered.

The boys huddled and crouched low, peering into the clearing through a small opening in the thicket, trying to see what was going on. But they could see only a part of the clearing and nothing was happening there.

The voices, however, were unmistakable. "Ha! Ha! Ha! D'you see 'em jump when the bullet hit 'em?"

"Yup! Musta' jumped three feet in the air."

"No wonder. Look where one bullet hit 'em." That remark was followed by thunderous laughter.

Huddled like scared rabbits, Ted and Roland glanced at each other.

"We better get outta' here!" Roland whispered urgently.

With fear gripping the boys, they bolted from their hiding place and began a desperate, charging run down Main Trail. The sudden commotion rustled the bushes.

"Hey, there's another one!" The shout came just before a shot rang out, followed by a sickening, terrorizing 'thuck' as the bullet buried itself into a tree trunk near the boys. A terrifying, deathly fear released in the boys a burst of energy that carried them along the trail at a speed never attained before. They disregarded the brushes, snags and scrapes as they zipped along the trail.

"Rolan', I'm scared!" Ted's voice quivered behind Roland.

"C'mon, keep runnin'!" Roland urged.

Eventually, they were far enough away from Big Swale so that the Brotchell voices faded. When the boys reached the security of the lake, totally exhausted, they collapsed, breathless, by the water's edge. For the next few minutes, they panted as they glanced at each other and looked around and shivered in fear and panted some more. Even after they recovered their strength and breath, they just sat on the ground, silently thinking over what they had just experienced. Finally, Ted spoke, his voice still reflecting some of the terror.

"I was really scared, Rolan'. I never been that scared." There followed a moment of silence. "I never wanna' see another Brothell again."

"Yeah! Me too."

The boys fell silent again. Then Roland stated soberly: "We better not tell Ma or Pa anythin' about this."

"Yeah," Ted agreed. "We'd prob'bly be banned from goin' to Big Swale ever again." Once more, silence prevailed around the lake area. Even the ducks paddled around as though unconcerned, only now and then quacking a protest or an announcement.

"I think you better give up this idea of a wild horse. You can get killed lookin' for 'em."

"But I want 'em."

"Sure you want 'em, but you see what you almost got out there." Ted felt a wave of bravery.

"Them Brotchells don't own Big Swale."

"No, they don't. But they don't care about who or what's in it...you saw that."

"Yeah, they really don't care about nothin'."

There followed a moment of close encounter, of touching spirits and of understanding that sets in when two or more human beings survive a challenge or disaster together. Sitting on the ground by the water, in the quiet and privacy offered by the lake, Ted and Roland experienced such a moment. This feeling of silent togetherness was good preparation for what was about to occur.

10

Christmas Eve

The contrast of the late December chill with the warm spirit of the corning season put a bounce into Ted's step. It was now just a few days before Christmas and Ted felt, as he had in the years before, a special difference–even an awe and wonder of this unique time of year. There was an anticipation, a real waiting, of an event Ted didn't really understand. Ma Crockett's explanation of a birth two thousand years ago, and the explanation he heard in church seemed to describe an event that occurred somewhere too far away in place and time but which mysteriously touched the present–even here, in the Crockett home.

Ted stood looking out the kitchen window and watched the car shrink down the road.

"Where's Pa goin'?" he asked his mother.

Ma Crockett assumed her annual, mysterious way and answered vaguely. "He's going to town to get flour and sugar so I can bake some sweets for Christmas." And bake she knew how, producing cakes and cookies and home-made candies which appeared only at Christmastime. Her baking would win gold ribbons at any fair.

"Need help with anythin'?" Ted offered, suspecting there would be an opportunity to lick pots and utensils clean of sweet scrapings. He also sensed that there was another reason for his father's trip to town and he happily made himself available for any chore. In the past, his offerings to help became a little pesky, to the point of nuisance, and Ma Crockett had to throw him out of the kitchen for the sake of her own peace and quiet.

"Why don't you sweep the livin' room floor…we'll be puttin' up the tree soon."

Ted liked orders that sounded more like suggestions, like requests. Any other time of the year, he would object and complain and make excuses, but the season held a spell over him, and he responded with an enthusiastic "Sure, Ma". There was willingness in his response that was obviously absent the rest of the year. Grabbing the worn straw broom from behind the kitchen door, he began swishing it across the plain, bare wood floor. In no time, he worked his way to the nook from which the tree would rule and he paused to allow a dream to float through his mind.

"Be sure to get in the corners an' back under the furniture," Ma Crockett called out. He thought his mother was so wise, knowing what he was doing even though she couldn't see him from the kitchen.

"O. K, Ma," he called back as he resumed working the broom, reaching under a chest into a far comer. As he pulled the broom forward, a sizable dust ball floated out. It must have occupied the corner for a long time–long enough to create its own little universe of dust wads.

Ted worked the broom over the entire living room floor, even under the potbelly stove, gathering dust balls from dark corners and hiding places. He was careful not to sweep too vigorously, though, lest the cloud of dust he might stir up, after settling on everything, become his next chore. So he carefully herded all the dust balls, grit, wood chips–even a marble, which he captured–into a little pile and scooped the little landscape into a dented, rusty dustpan. Carefully handling the dustpan, he dumped the contents into the trash can, clanging the pan to proclaim the end of his chore. "I'm goin' outside now, Ma," he announced as he hung the broom back on its nail behind the kitchen door.

"Don't go too far. We're goin' to eat when Pa comes back." As Ted donned his jacket, she added, "maybe this afternoon, why don't you clean the mud room?"

Again, there was that request that normally would have drawn protests and excuses, but his mother's timing worked again and the 'sure, Ma' reached her just before the sound of the closing door.

Ted stepped out into the chill morning. Roland came out of the house behind him.

"Where you goin'?" he asked.

"Thought I'd get some more firewood and stack it on the porch before it rains or somethin' ."

Falling in step, the brothers set out for the woodpile. "Been thinkin' about what you want for Christmas?" Roland asked.

"Yeah!" Immediately, Ted's mind shifted into high speed visualize. "I really want my own horse again. But there's a lotta' stuff in the catalog I want, too."

"Yeah! Me, too."

The boys silently dreamed the rest of the way to the woodpile. Each loaded an arm- full of logs and took it back to the house, all in a dreamy silence. Even the geese that flew overhead did not distract them.

It was now just three days to Christmas Day but, to Ted, it seemed like the whole year was yet to pass. During these holidays from school, he spent much time thinking about things: the wild horse; Spectrum (the one destroyed and the one escaped); his brother Gene out in the Pacific, wherever that was; and Wanda. There was also time to play Christmas songs on his harmonica and he played while walking around the lake or sitting by the barn. He knew only a few of the standard songs, mostly those he learned in school and in church. He was not allowed to turn on the radio–it was somehow like a sacred box to be touched only by his father or Roland - and the belly of the old Victrola record player held not a single Christmas record.

But many times, Ted just played whatever inspiration he seemed to hear in his head.

He actually composed and memorized a tune and, visualizing a place far to the north where snow was a part of winter, matched some words to it. He began to sing to himself:

"Snowflakes resting on my window sill, Christmas bells echo–echo–'cross the distant hills... ." He played an interlude, then continued:" *...where children play, and sleigh bells ring, an' the hills an' trees are covered with sparkling snow.* "He always insured that no one heard him as he felt shy about others hearing him play and sing.

On Christmas Eve, as evening approached, Ted stayed near the house as though he was tied there like a puppy. His mother was preparing the Christmas Eve supper, a most solemn and awe-inspiring meal. Later, as mealtime approached, Ted would make himself available for special and delightful chores.

"Ted, wanna' give me a hand with the tree?"

"Sure, Pa," Ted answered with that bounce in his step. "Can I pick it out this year?"

"We'll see," Pa Crockett responded with fatherly authority, for he always chose when and which tree would be cut. No one questioned his decision, even during this mellow season. Now, father, a saw in his hand, and son, a gleam in his eye, approached the row of salt cedars that lined the north side of the house like a sprawling shield against wintry winds. Roland joined them and the three paced around with upturned faces, studying the shapes of the branches, searching for one with a yuletide form. The Christmas tree would not actually be a tree. Rather, a branch from one of the large trees would become the 'tree' of the season.

"Here's one, Pa," Ted indicated.

Pa Crockett gave it a studied look. "Umm!" he grunted "How about this one?"

"Umm!"

Ted and Roland pointed out others, but in the end it was Pa Crockett who decided which branch was the right one and he cut it ceremoniously.

"Looks real fine, Pa." Ted looked over the branch which was about his own height- maybe a little more - and had enough branches to give it a squat appearance. Course, string-like leaves hung from the branches and swayed and waved in unison as Ted carried the tree to the house.

"Go ahead and put it up," Pa Crockett directed.

Ted and Roland carefully wrestled the tree into the house and attached a stand to the base. After some positioning, it stood in its place of honor, almost as wide as it was talL Its stringy leaves hung down like short pieces of twine, and the pungent aroma of the cut wood, and of the tree itself, began to fill the room.

As the boys stepped back to check the tree, a smiling Ma Crockett entered the room carrying a box of decorations which had adorned the Crockett tree for the past two decades. "That's a nice tree," she observed as she opened the box, releasing pent-up odors of age and repeated use. "You boys ready to decorate?"

"I'll do the candles," Ted announced. While Roland and Ma Crockett hung tinsels and ornaments, Ted pressed stubby candles, left over from previous years, into clip-on candle holders sticky with the wax of many Christmases. Grabbing a handful of stringy leaves, he clipped on the whole assembly.

"Be sure the candles sit straight up," Ma Crockett advised. Ted quickly corrected one that was leaning badly. "An' make sure the flames will be clear of the tree so we don't bum the house down," she cautioned further.

Soon, the transformation of a plain cedar branch into a twinkling, colorful Christmas tree was complete. They all stepped back and, as the awe and magic worked its way into their hearts, the beauty and magic of the season reflected in three beaming faces.

"Sure is pretty," Ma Crockett sighed softly.

"Sure is," the boys agreed in chorus, grinning satisfaction.

The sound of a closing door signaled the arrival of Pa Crockett. Seeing the tree all decked out, he smiled that half smile of his. "Didn't waste any time, didja'?" he chuckled.

"How's it look, Pa?' Ted gushed, searching for a compliment.

"Well, looks just aw'right," he replied in his restrained manner, as though afraid to actually give a compliment.

By now, Ma Crockett was kneeling at the base of the tree, arranging the manger scene by positioning plaster figurines, chipped and scarred from years of adoration. The three wise men, however, remained in the box since, true to her understanding of the event, they would arrive later, on the feast of the Epiphany. By then, the first week of January would have passed and the tree would be gone, leaving the manger scene all alone. But the figurines of the three wise men would be added on the day of Epiphany and would remain on display another week or so before the whole scene would be packed away to hibernate until next December.

The manger scene completed, Ma Crockett lifted herself off her knees, boosted by a slight groan. She left the room and came back with wrapped presents, placing them carefully under the tree. Then she said: "Ted, how about helpin' me finish supper?"

"Sure, Ma," he replied in true holiday spirit.

"Here's the tablecloth." Ma Crockett said, handing it to him.

Ted reached out for the special tablecloth, used only on this occasion or Easter or when the pastor of the church carne to dinner. He felt the smooth, soft fabric–almost silky–and fingered the course embroidery around the border, made by his mother's own hands. The cloth itself was the whitest fabric in the house, much whiter than bed sheets or towels. Ted sensed the specialness of it as he reverently spread it over the table.

Next, he opened the china cabinet and studied the stack of plates.

"Careful you don't break any dishes," Ma Crockett cautioned. This was her very best china, some of it handed down from her mother, and she allowed its use only on these special occasions–just like the table cloth. Ted carefully lifted four plates out of the cabinet and glided his fingers over the textured edge, over the flowery pattern on the rim and down into the center of the plate, smooth and shiny with a single flower beneath the glaze. He set each plate down gingerly. Next to each one, he aligned the silverware that his mother had brought out: shiny, smooth and special, like the plates and the table cloth.

Finally, each plate received a portion of Christmas condiments, the only time of the year this arrangement appeared on the Crockett dinner table. These were: an apple, an orange, a tangerine, and a little mound of nuts which included pecans, walnuts, filberts, Brazil nuts, and almonds - all snug in their shells. Next to all this, in a place of honor, Ted added some candy. A small folded paper bag completed the setting.

"All set, Ma," he announced.

His mother didn't even look up from her cooking. "Get a slice of bread and cut it into four squares," she ordered. "An' cut off the crust ... an' set out the honey."

With the table now ready, bowls of food were transferred from the stove to the table.

As lids were lifted on the containers, little curls and plumes of steam rose from the hot pots and wispy streams of aromas intertwined and wafted through the house. After all gathered at the table, Pa Crockett led in the saying of grace. Even the grace was different tonight as he added some words to the usual prayer. Afterwards, dipping a spoon into the honey, he laced the four squares of bread with the string of honey oozing off the spoon.

In silence, everyone took a square and, as they ate–reverently–Ma Crockett addressed Ted. "Do you remember why we do this?" Usually, she explained the symbolism herself.

Ted always felt shy talking about religious things and he shifted nervously in his seat.

Clearing his throat, he began. "One day, the Christ child got lost while playing and He was lying hungry under a bush and bees came and put honey on His lips to feed Him." Ted wasn't sure that's what really had happened, but it made a nice story. Ma Crockett had assured him last year, when he had asked about it, that the story was true and that it had come down through generations of her family.

"We eat honey on bread to commemorate this miracle," Ma Crockett concluded.

Ted was glad when the commemorative ritual was over and he joined the others in the most solemn eating of the year.

Between bites, Ma Crockett intoned religiously, "We're thankful for this meal an' all that we have. An' we also remember Eugene, an' give thanks for his safety," she concluded with a quiver in her voice. No one else spoke during the meal, partly due to the solemnity and partly because of the good food. Ted was grateful for the silence for he felt uneasy mixing religion and eating. He did miss his oldest brother, but the good food helped soothe the memory.

"This is real good pie, Ma," Ted finally said as he stuffed the last empty corner of his stomach with a piece that had a filling measuring three fingers high and was topped with fluffy, frothy beaten egg whites sprinkled with shredded cocoanut. Then, he wasted no time in examining his little hill of Christmas goodies. Popping a piece of candy into this mouth, he ruffled his paper bag and put the fruit and goodies in as though they were gold nuggets. The bulging bag would accompany him everywhere for the next day or two until all that it contained was gone.

Observing that everyone had finished eating, Pa Crockett rose wordlessly from the table, a signal for all to go into the living room. There, Ted and Roland lit the candles on the tree. The tinsel and ornaments sparkled the reflections of the flames, while the cedar leaves hung like subdued strings.

Pa Crockett reached up and dimmed the kerosene lantern, and the family stepped back to behold the scene–a true picture of Christmas. Aromas of burning wax floated throughout the room on wisps of smoke while friendly shadows danced on the wall near the tree.

The hush and stillness reached an unbearable point when, at last, Ma Crockett's voice broke the silence. She led the family to its knees and intoned a prayer of thanksgiving. As every year, she became emotional and wept at the inspiring scene. Pa Crockett knelt solemnly, head bowed, arms hanging in front with his fingers clasped and entwined. Roland studied the tree and all the presents around it. Ted was completely awestruck, reacting to the emotional charge with an open mouth half-smile, his eyes sparkling like the candles on the tree. This was a sacred moment, a hallowed few minutes that created four distinct worlds, yet united all four in one common feeling and belief. No other moment throughout the year equaled this one in solemnity, inspiration, love and closeness.

"Amen," everyone intoned at the end of Ma Crockett's prayer.

"An' we ask that you bring Gene back soon," she added. "Amen," the others responded again. Another short and pious moment followed before they all rose, slowly and silently, except Pa Crockett, who needed the assistance of a groan to get up.

"Ted, why don't you see what's under the tree?" To the sound of chairs scooting across the wooden floor, Ted fell to one knee and, picking up the presents one at a time, he tilted them toward the candlelight, read the names and distributed the gifts. Everyone immediately opened presents, carefully untying the ribbons and gently unwrapping the paper. These would be saved to enfold treasured gifts next Christmas.

With the rustle of paper, the mood in the room changed and Pa Crockett boosted the lantern. The increased light revealed more clearly the contents of the wrappings: new overalls for Pa; a new scarf for Ma to wear to church. Roland received a new shirt and a notebook binder to replace the tattered one he now carried to school, and a pair of socks. Ted found a pair of socks and a cardboard punch-out airplane kit…and a new harmonica! He accepted the other gifts with calm enthusiasm, but the harmonica lit a fire.

"Wow!…Hey! Look, everybody!…Look at this…Look what I got!" His face glowed as he showed it around like it was the only present in the house.

"That's a very nice gift, Ted," Ma Crockett enthused.

"Yeah, Ted, now you can really play," Roland added. "Maybe you'll play somethin' now."

Pa Crockett said nothing, but smiled knowingly as he gave Ted a teasing rub on the head.

"Can you play us somethin'?" Ma Crockett asked.

Ted liked being the center of attention, but felt uneasy and shy about playing in front of anybody.

Roland coaxed: "C'mon, Ted. Let's hear somethin'."

Bashfully, Ted raised the harmonica to his lips and blew softly. The new, pliant reeds vibrated easily and smoothly, producing rich, mellow tones. He played a few notes, caressing the harmonica in his hands and smoothly sliding his tongue and lips over the new shiny metal and varnished wood. Such beautiful sounds were most worthy of his own song. He closed his eyes, inhaled and, with a breath like a whisper, played a few bars, mentally singing: *'snowflakes resting on my window sill, Christmas bells echo...echo...cross the distant hills...'* Shyness overtook him at this point and he lowered the harmonica, savoring the taste of the new instrument, and examined it in an attempt to hide his embarrassment.

"That was nice, Ted," Ma Crockett complimented. "Wish there was more music here tonight."

"Better blow out the candles," Pa Crockett ordered. Wax was dripping onto the floor and more than one candle was getting very stubby. Ted and Roland jumped to the task, respectfully blowing out a candle here and a candle there until all were extinguished. They most likely would not be re-lit until next Christmas.

"Someone's comin'! Ma Crockett exclaimed, observing car lights through the kitchen window. Everyone rushed to the window.

"Who'd be comin' tonight?" Pa Crockett questioned, unhappy with the intrusion. The vehicle was approaching slowly, stopping now and then.

"Looks like a pickup," Roland announced as they all bunched up around the window and peered out.

Suddenly, Ted exclaimed: "Looks like the Brotchell pickup!"

"What the devil do they want here tonight?" Pa Crockett growled in an un-Christmas like manner.

They all huddled anxiously as the lights turned and came straight toward the house. "Sure looks like a pickup," Roland reaffirmed, studying the parts of the grill and bumper lit up by the headlights. "Could be the Brotchells," he added.

As the vehicle arrived at the front of the house, everyone switched windows to the one facing the front. They all got into position just as the vehicle stopped. The lights stayed on, shining at the house. Then they heard the sound of a door slamming. Seconds later, a figure emerged out of the darkness at the side of the lights.

"It's a girl!" Roland exclaimed

"What the devil does she want here?" Pa Crockett growled softly.

The slim, tall and straight figure came forward and stopped inside the lighted area in front of the headlights. A memory of a tall and straight girl standing on a porch flashed through Ted's mind, and he blurted out: "It's the Brotchell girl!"

"What devil brings her here?" Pa Crockett growled again, still in an un-Christmas like tone.

Ma Crockett whispered, "Wonder what she wants?"

The girl took a few halting steps forward. She was tall and straight, a dark figure against the glaring headlights. "Go see what she wants," Pa Crockett directed.

"I'll go," Ma Crockett answered, "but you keep watchin'."

Under the watchful gaze of three pairs of eyes in the window, Ma Crockett stepped out onto the porch.

The figure spoke. "Can I talk to you?" The voice was calm, ringing with a kind of clarity that reflected class and breeding. It hardly seemed that she could be a product of the Brotchell household.

Ma Crockett stepped down off the porch and the figure took a few more steps forward, glancing back into the darkness behind the headlights.

"What do you want here?" Ma Crockett asked firmly, "especially this evenin'...what do you want?"

The figure stepped forward again. "My brother is in the pickup," the voice began, clearly and calmly. "He doesn't want to be here and he doesn't want me to be here, but I come as a friend...please let me talk to you." Even the request was calm and unwavering, and the figure stood still.

"Step over to the side so I can see your face." Ma Crockett's eyes followed the slim figure's halting steps into a changing angle of light and saw it transform into the person of the girl. The shifted view revealed a chiseled, long face framed by straight shoulder- length hair. "We don't even know you here...what's your name?"

The girl remained unemotional and her response was a while in coming. When it did, it was slow and clear. "My name is Melany Brotchell." She stood as still as a pillar.

Ma Crockett leaned forward, peering into the girl's expressionless face–long, with pronounced features, wide set eyes hardened in place and a slice of thin, firm lips beneath a pointed nose. "Melany Brotchell," Ma Crockett repeated. "We don't think much of your family here, but you're actually a very pretty girl." She moved up to Melany until they were at arm's length. What's that on the side of your face?"

Melany raised a long, slender arm and covered her cheek, but she remained composed and tall and expressionless. "That's where my Pa slapped me," she revealed calmly.

Ma Crockett jerked back from the shock of the straight answer. She glanced at the window that framed three faces. "It took a lotta' courage for you to come here."

A voice from behind the headlights called out, "Melany, hurry up. Let's go." Melany glanced back toward the lights. "Not yet, big brother," she called back.

Ma Crockett's nervousness began to show. "Melany, I don't understand why you're here. Your brother sounds pretty...pretty mean."

Melany shifted on her feet, but remained tall and composed. "Does a slap from your Pa bring you here?"

The quiet of the night was no match for the silence of the girl whose beauty and manner were so out of context with the character of her family. "My Pa wants me to be a boy," she finally said calmly. "He wants me to ride horses...to spit...to shoot guns...to act like my brothers."

"C'mon, Melany, let's go," the voice from the truck beckoned again, impatiently. "Just a little while longer, big brother," she called back.

In her confused uneasiness, Ma Crockett asked, "an' you don't want to ride horses or even shoot a pistol?"

"Not one bit...never!"

"How old are you, Melany?"

"I'm fifteen, almost sixteen."

"Well, you're a grown-up fifteen."

"C'mon, Melany," the voice demanded loudly. This time, Melany ignored the command, seeming to draw confidence from this woman so unlike her own mother.

"What do you want from us? Why did you come?"

The tall, steady figure of Melany Brotchell took a deep breath, squinted the wide-set eyes slightly and fixed them on the woman she was beginning to like. "I watched my brothers bring your husband out of the woods and load him into that truck after they shot him." She paused as the tension further electrified the evening. "I watched my brothers have their fun with your son when he got hurt in our corral...and then they mistreated his horse even though he already had a broken leg." Her voice maintained its steadiness and reserve, and she stood motionless, still showing no emotion. "I watched them beat up horses and other animals they could catch, just for fun."

During the tense pause that followed, Ma Crockett wrinkled her face and breathed a whisper: "Why are you tellin' me this?"

"Melany!" the voice from behind the pickup called again, more forcefully and in a higher pitch, accompanied by the sound of the truck door opening. Again, Melany ignored the demand.

"I cannot be like my brothers," she continued bravely. "My Pa pushes me around and sometimes he pushes me out the door and drags me to the corral to be with the horses and he cusses at me... ." Her voice remained composed, but it softened and a slight waver appeared. "I don't want that to happen anymore."

"Melany, there's really nothin' we can do to change any of that," Ma Crockett sympathized. "There's no way we can interfere in your family. Why have you come here to tell us this?"

Melany's heroic composure firmed up her voice. "This afternoon, my Pa took me to the corral and gave me one of the horses and said it was my Christmas present.

"I told him that I didn't want it and we had an argument–we're never supposed to talk back to Pa–and he slapped me real hard...and hit me in other places." She lowered her eyes momentarily.

"Melany..." Ma Crockett was at a loss for what to say, and a long silence ensued as the two figures stood in the night, eyes riveted on each other in a kind of mother-daughter bond.

Finally, without shifting her gaze, Melany spoke. "There's a horse tied to the back of the pickup...the one my Pa gave me. I have no use for it. I don't want it. I don't want to feed it or care for it or anything."

"Hurry up, Melany!" the voice from the pickup shouted angrily.

Unaffected, Melany continued. "I want your son to have it. Maybe it can replace the one he had before…the one my brothers…" Her voice choked on the words and, for the first time, Melany Brotchell showed emotion. She tried to continue but the quiver in her chin would not let her form the words. She remained straight and tall and stood still as teardrops formed and ran down her cheeks, glistening in the light from the headlights.

"Melany, we cannot accept your horse. There would never be… ."

"Please," Melany interrupted with a sniff. Let me leave him here." She inhaled deeply,

"My brothers would only have fun with him now that he's supposed to be mine." During the pause that followed, she recovered her control and composure and her voice regained its original ring. "Please take him. I want your son to have him." Then, abruptly and without another word, she turned and strode back toward the truck.

Ma Crockett stood dumbfounded as the tall, slim figure disappeared into the darkness behind the headlights. She heard some shuffling in the darkness. Then, two doors slammed, the engine revved up and, as the truck circled the yard to leave, the side glow of the headlights revealed a horse tied to the mulberry tree.

As the truck departed, Pa Crockett, followed by Roland–flashlight in hand–and Ted emerged from the house. The dim glow from the living room window cast a shadow of Ma Crockett standing in the night, stunned by the event that had just taken place.

"What was all that?" Pa Crockett wanted to know as he stepped off the porch.

A snort punctuated the night and Roland searched with the flashlight beam, locking it on the horse tied to the mulberry tree.

"What's that doin' there?" Pa Crockett demanded.

Ma Crockett did not answer. She did not even move from her position of final encounter with Melany Brotchell. But Roland and Ted immediately set out to inspect the horse. It greeted them with another snort as they approached.

Roland played the flashlight beam over the horse's body: head held high with questioning ears...neck...shoulders...side...rump..."Look here, Ted," he called out in surprise.

Before Ted even got close, he recognized the familiar markings. "Spectrum!" he gasped. "Spectrum!" he repeated as he flung his arms around the horse's neck. "Ma, Pa, come look!" he called out.

Pa Crockett rushed over. "What you got, Ted?"

"Look, Pa," Ted bubbled. "This is the same horse we captured two months ago. The one you said I couldn't keep...the one that disappeared from the lake!"

While Ted hugged and squeezed and petted the horse's head and neck, his parents and brother watched in astonishment and disbelief.

Ma Crockett broke the spell softly. "I don't understand why any of this happened. I just don't understand anythin' that happened out here tonight.

Pa Crockett ordered, though mildly: "You boys put 'em up in the pen for the night," as he turned and started walking back toward the house.

Ma Crockett went alongside. "She seemed like such a sensitive girl."

"Still a Brotchell," snorted Pa Crockett.

"There must be some terrible things goin' on in that household," Ma Crockett proposed.

"What you expect? They're Brotchells."

Ma Crockett suggested: "Maybe, since it's Christmas, we could change our feelin's about 'em a little bit.

Pa Crockett didn't answer right away. "Caint raise no argument with that...but they'll always be Brotchells an' they don't deserve any consideration."

"Yeah, but it's Christmas and there's supposed to be somethin' about lovin' your neighbor" .

Pa Crockett reached down and found Ma Crockett's hand. As they entered the house, a whinny and a shout, coming from the direction of the pen, dispelled whatever quiet was left of what was supposed to be a silent night. Another whinny and more laughter came from the pen.

"Better get the boys inside," Ma Crockett advised, "or they'll spend the night out there with that horse…an' there's church in the mornin'."

As Pa Crockett turned to retrieve the boys, Ma Crockett added, "we'll prob'bly have to pry Ted away from that animal in the mornin' anyway."

11

Christmas Day

Christmas morning was peaceful and quiet. Ted awoke easily. His night had been one of light sleep which had come slowly after the dramatic events of the previous evening. Fitful dreams interrupted his slumber several times and each time he got up and made his way, shivering in the dark cold, to the window to peer outside. Each time, only the blackness of the night stared back at him. Once, he saw a shooting star. But each time, he made his way back to his bed and, snuggling into the lingering warmth he had left in the featherbed, tried to fall asleep.

As the morning sun prepared to dissolve the cold darkness, Ted rose from his bed, slipped on his cold pants and shirt and, bundling up in his jacket, stole out of the house. Spectrum was lying on a bed of old hay, his back against the barn. He raised his head as Ted approached the gate.

"G'mornin' there, Spectrum," he said as he climbed over the gate and proceeded toward the horse, which was now getting up. He rubbed Spectrum's nose and Spectrum bumped Ted's chest, pushing him backward. Giggling, Ted ran around to the side and, grabbing a handful of mane, flipped himself onto the horse's back. After riding a circle in the pen, he dismounted to open the gate, led Spectrum out and remounted, setting a course for the lake. Both horse and boy puffed miniature clouds of frosty breath along the way. At the lake, as the few eastern clouds held on to their pink lining, Ted absorbed himself in his dream come true. Even the quacking of the Christmas morning ducks and the geese overhead failed to distract him and he spent an intimate hour with his returned friend, riding this way and that just for fun.

"Hey, Ted, you gonna' live out there?"

The voice seemed far away, but Ted looked toward the woodpile and saw Roland waving and calling. He acknowledged his brother with a grinning wave.

"Gonna' be time for church pretty soon," Roland called. "Ma says to come in already." Roland's announcement was heard across the lake and all the way to the woods, carried on the Christmas morning stillness. Ted responded by turning his horse toward the pen.

The church service, festive on this day, held little festivity for Ted. One difference was that there were more people and Ted had to sit squeezed between two boys. And there was more singing than usual. A large manger scene, with the figurines about two feet tall, positioned on real hay, was also an addition. The familiar was there, too. Wanda sat squeezed between two girls on the other side of the aisle and she and Ted exchanged smiles when their eyes met. After the service, when families engaged in short visits, Ted and Roland visited with Chris and Wanda.

Ted bubbled: "You shoulda' seen what happened last night. Real strange. This Brotchell girl comes over in the dark an' leaves this horse for me. An' its the same horse I been feedin' out at the lake, the one that disappeared."

"Why'd she do that?" Chris wanted to know.

"It was real spooky. Ma said the girl got it for Christmas an' didn't want it."

"So, will you be able to keep 'em?" Wanda asked.

"Yeah. I think so, 'cause she told my Ma that it was for me 'cause she didn't want it an' 'cause her brothers did all that stuff to my horse."

Roland added: "It really was strange. The Brotchells had some kinda' fight or somethin' and the girl forced one of her brothers to bring her an' the horse. They came in the pickup, in the dark, with the horse tied to the back of the pickup. It was strange."

"Yeah," Ted continued. "The horse wasn't beat up or nothin', but Ma said the girl had some kinda' sore spots on her, where someone hit her."

"Maybe we can see your horse this afternoon," Wanda suggested.

"Yeah. We're comin' over," Chris added as they parted. "I'm bringin' some firecrackers," he threw back over his shoulder. "See ya'," Ted and Roland said in chorus and waved.

Shortly after dinner, Ted was back at the lake, astride Spectrum, his bag of Christmas Eve goodies between his knees. He let the horse wander about as he munched on the nuts and candy–a picture of contentment. Earlier, Spectrum had accepted his offer of the apple.

When the Bereneks arrived, the three boys wasted no time engaging in shooting firecrackers in the field just beyond the cedar trees, away from the house. Wanda stayed back and watched Roland put a firecracker into a tin can, thread the wick through a hole in the bottom and shove the inverted can into the soft earth. "Watch it go," he yelled as he lit the wick. "Stand back!" The explosion was little more than a pop, but it shot the can higher than the trees. The boys hollered in delight as Chris packed a firecracker into a ball of dirt, lit the wick and hurled the ball into the air. "Look out!" he yelled just as the firecracker exploded overhead, sending bits of dirt in all directions, like a grenade. The boys laughed as they all ducked in defense. Soon, the place sounded like a battlefield with tin cans flying and balls of dirt exploding in the air.

With Wanda watching, it didn't take long for Ted to tire of the sport. "Wanna' go ride my horse?"

"Sure!"

He felt a surge of warmth at her quick reply. "Can you ride today...I mean, you're wearin' a dress an'... ." Ted began to feel uncomfortable and wished he had not asked.

"Sure, I can ride." A flush on her face accompanied her bashful reply.

Without so much as a glance back at Roland and Chris, still absorbed in firecracker games, Ted and Wanda left to go to the pen to see Spectrum. On the way, as they passed by the Berenek car, Wanda said, "Just a minute." She opened a rear door, reached into the back seat and pulled out an irregularly shaped present.

"Here. I brought you somethin' for Christmas."

Ted's face reddened with embarrassment. "What is it?"

"Open it."

Ted suddenly felt a heaviness in the pit of his stomach. "Shucks, Wanda, I don't have nothin' for you."

"Sure you do," she encouraged. "You're gonna' let me ride your horse." She smiled at him. "Now, go ahead. Open it."

Ted carefully unfolded the wrapping, just like he had on the presents the night before.

From the folds emerged a red cap which sported an uncommonly long bill.

"Hope it fits," Wanda smiled proudly, "I thought you could wear it when you ride your horse."

Ted slapped the cap into shape and flipped it onto a head of disheveled hair, some of which stuck out from underneath the cap like an oriental roof. But his face glowed with satisfaction under the comically long bill. "It fits O.K." he announced gleefully as he took it off, examined it and flipped it back onto his head, once again forming oriental roofs. He felt as spirited as the wild horse. "Wanna' ride Spectrum now?"

"Sure"

They proceeded to the pen and entered as Ted politely held the gate open. Spectrum was at the far side, a place hidden from the house by the barn. Ted noted the seclusion and, feeling a familiar tingle, looked at Wanda. She returned the gaze, adding a smile. Impulsively, they yielded to an invisible force that closed the distance, and their lips touched–barely. The act was comically hidden by the long bill of Ted's cap. They drew back immediately as though the contact had been accidental, like brushing against someone in a crowded school hallway. But there were two guilty smiles on two guilty faces as Ted and Wanda exchanged brief glances, like Culprits catching each other in their own misdeeds.

Wanda just stood smiling, but Ted struggled to turn his attention to Spectrum. Not completely attentive to the task, he fumbled for Spectrum's harness and led the horse around to present its side to Wanda.

"How am I gonna' get on his back?" she asked meekly.

Ted puzzled over this point and realized how ridiculous it was to expect Wanda to leap onto Spectrum's back the way he did. After pondering a moment, he offered a solution. "I'll get Spectrum over next to the fence an' you can climb on the fence an' get on his back." With the horse in position, Ted respectfully looked away as Wanda, in a flurry of skirt, legs and bloomers, performed an awkward climb onto the fence and an even more awkward shift onto the horse's back.

"I did it," she announced triumphantly as she wiggled and settled on Spectrum's back, bloomers peeking out from under her skirt. She looked at the arrangement, blushed and looked at Ted. He pretended not to see.

"Wanna' ride to the lake?"

"Sure."

Ted led the horse out of the gate and around the barn, by the chicken coop, past the woodpile and on to the lake.

"This feels funny...it feels wobbly...like rockin' in a crooked rockin' chair." Wanda wiggled around a bit, trying for more comfort.

"Are you scared?"

"Just a little."

"Don't be scared. You're aw'right an' I won't let Spectrum run or nothin', an' you can stay on as long as he just walks like this. Hold on to his mane."

"His what?"

"The long hair on the back of his neck."

"Oh!"

As they rounded the far side of the lake, Ted pointed. "I seen a wild horse right over there."

"When?"

"Oh, a coupla' months ago. An' just a coupla' weeks ago, I seen 'em in the clearing in the woods."

"How do you know he's wild?"

Ted nodded his head up and down vigorously, the long bill on his new cap making funny arcs in front of his face. "Oh, I know!" he boasted confidently. "You shoulda' seen 'em, Wanda. I never seen a horse like 'em."

"Can I get off now, Ted?"

"Well, yeah, if you don't wanna' ride no more."

"How am I gonna' get down?"

Ted thought for a moment. "You can slide off...I won't look..., I'll be on the other side of the horse."

"It looks scary. Better hold my hands so I don't just tumble down."

"Wait! There's a tree stump over there. You can slide onto it, it'll be easier." Leading the horse to the stump, Ted positioned him alongside. Going to the opposite side, he offered his assistance. "Gim'me your hands." He weakened a little at the touch.

Positioning herself across Spectrum's back and holding on to Ted's hands, Wanda slid down toward the stump. "I'm glad you're not on this side," she said bashfully as her dress rode up to present the full show of underwear. "I did it!" she announced happily as she hopped off the stump and ruffled herself together. "What's that?" she asked, pointing toward the water.

"Aw, I tried to make a sailboat. It don't really look like a boat. It's just a piece of board ... an' I put a sail on it."

Wanda picked up the contraption. It was no more than a piece of two- by-four with slender pieces of wood nailed to each side and a piece of cloth–looked like a handkerchief–stretched between them. "Does it float?"

"Well, kinda'."

Wanda sat down on the bank as though preparing to watch the show and handed the sailboat to Ted. "Let's see," she challenged.

Ted couldn't resist the opportunity to show off. He set the sailboat on the water and immediately, it settled low, almost submerging. With the first puff of wind, the sail filled and the contraption leaned over on its side. "Really wasn't a very good idea," he explained.

Wanda giggled. "What else do you do out here?"

Ted sat down a polite distance from her. "Aw…goof aroun' a lot, ride my horse, go into the woods, watch the geese an' ducks, and play my harmonica."

Wanda jumped at the clue. "Lem'me hear you play," she begged.

"Aw, I'm not that good," Ted answered bashfully. "I just like to play when I'm by myself."

"Why?"

"Dunne. Just don't like no one to hear, I guess."
"You don't even want me to hear?" Wanda smiled.

Ted looked at her. She sat cross-legged, like a swami, and her skirt draped over her knees and billowed out around her. The sight of her made it difficult to refuse her request. Reaching into his pocket, he pulled out his new harmonica and showed it to Wanda. "I got this for Christmas, too," he said, offering the instrument for inspection.

"Sure feels smooth. Lem'me hear you play it," she repeated, handing it back.

Ted looked at her and her smile clicked on something in him, like a switch. Mouthing the harmonica, he closed his eyes and pictured a scene of snow-covered hills in a faraway land and a sled ride across the foothills–maybe with Wanda at his side. Drawing a deep breath, he serenaded her while mentally singing to himself: *Snowflakes resting on my window sill. Christmas bells echo–echo–cross the distant hills.*

Wanda peered at him, grinning at the way he wrinkled his face while he played. She liked the way he got involved with his song, the way the mellow tune filled the air like leaves floating to the ground. As the music coiled around them sitting on the bank, Wanda also closed her eyes and absorbed the melody which, like a silver yarn, wove a silky lace of ecstasy around them. By the time the last notes faded on the delicate film which they had spun, Wanda was totally entranced.

For a moment, the two figures sat in silence with their eyes still closed. The rapture dissolved slowly and Wanda opened her eyes just as Ted was opening his, struggling with her emotions.

"That was real good, Ted. I really liked it. I didn't know…ah…you never told me you could play like that."

Ted blushed a little. "I play best when I'm by myself."

"You're not by yourself now, an' you played real good."

"Yeah, but this was different."

Wanda turned to smile at him again but a voice from the woodpile interrupted.

"Hey, you want any lunch?" Roland called. "There's some cake an' other good stuff in the kitchen. Ma says to come on. Everybody's eatin."

Ted and Wanda looked at each other, silently agreed and rose from the bank. Ted got Spectrum and, with Wanda by his side, walked the horse back to the pen. But they did not speak until Spectrum was in the pen and Ted had closed the gate. By then, Ted felt the pressure to say something–anything. The silence was making him nervous. As they walked toward the house, he said: "My Ma makes some pretty good cake." Immediately, he felt stupid for making such a remark.

"I'm really not hungry... ."

"I sorta' am... ."

At the table, both statements proved correct. In fact, Ted accepted seconds of the pastries as they were offered. Soon everyone was full, the conversation lagged and the Bereneks began to leave, an event which always echoed with large amounts of laughter that never seemed to end until the car was on its way down the road.

Ted watched them leave and felt an emptiness as the car disappeared–like the end of Christmas day and the departure of the Bereneks somehow conspired to create a vacuum in his heart. He wished he could stop time and get himself stuck in the good parts of life.

Confused, he went up to his room and laid down on the bed to think and remember and dream. Soon, he began feeling good feelings.

Evening came much too quickly. Prodded by a sense of responsibility, he reluctantly performed his chores of milking and feeding and watering. With the sun touching the tree tops on its way to bidding the day farewell, Ted again mounted Spectrum and set out for the lake, proudly wearing his new cap.

"He still looks like a board," Pa Crockett joked to Roland as they walked toward the house, glancing back at Ted. "except now," he chuckled with delight, "he looks like he's got a roof off one side."

"Yeah, he does," Roland laughed in agreement.

Ma Crockett met them at the front porch. "Where's Ted goin'?"

"To the lake, looks like," Roland answered as he continued on into the house.

Ma Crockett waited until Roland was inside, then lowered her voice to Pa Crockett.

"Ted should not be alone with Wanda so much, 'specially out at the lake. You oughta' talk to 'em about it."

Pa Crockett cleared his throat nervously and tightened one side of his mouth. Without saying a word, he made a meaningless journey around to the side of the house. Ma Crockett went inside.

When Ted found the place where he and Wanda had sat that afternoon, he dismounted and walked to it. As the sky took on the first yellowish tint of the sunset, he sat down in his favorite chin-on-knees position and fixed his usual stare into the water. He remained this way until the sky began to fade from orange to pink.

Suddenly, Spectrum snorted; Ted jerked out of his thoughts as a whinny arrived from the north edge of the woods. He jumped up, peering in the direction of the sound. There, the waning light of the sunset glistened off the black coat of a horse, and Ted's feelings went from wonder to bewilderment to satisfaction. "It's the wild horse," he whispered to Spectrum. The round face of the twelve year old boy now reflected joy and elation. "It's the wild horse," he whispered again. Impulsively, he swung himself onto Spectrum's back and, with a squeeze of his knees, commanded: "C'mon, Spectrum! Let's go see 'em!"

The black horse immediately whinnied a warning. Spectrum snorted back. But Ted had no time for indecision or fear. "C'mon, boy, let's go see!" he said, giving his horse another squeeze of his knees. Spectrum shifted into a trot and Ted gripped the jostling mane lightly, excitement rushing through his body. But, when they had gone about half the distance, close enough so Ted could really see the horse's black coat, long flowing mane, sharp ears and long trailing tail; just when he was getting close enough to see the outlines of bulging muscles and flaring nostrils, the black horse shook its head, whinnied, spun around and trotted off into the woods.

"Whoa, Spectrum, whoa!" Feeling the pain of failure and realizing that it was useless to follow because of the increasing darkness, Ted let Spectrum stand while he gazed into the spot where the horse had vanished. "That really was the wild one," he informed Spectrum. "I knew there was a wild one all along." He took off his red cap and slapped it against his leg. "Doggone it, I was right!" Boosted by this renewed confidence, he spun Spectrum around as another whinny floated out of the woods. He looked back and, giving Spectrum free rein, he engaged his imagination and entered his dream. Out of the recesses of his mind floated a vision of streaking speed, smooth stretching grace, glistening black hide; out of a deep niche in his mind came a dream from back in 1941 when he was ten years old, a dream that lit the desire for horse ownership. For the moment, memories of Wanda and the dreamlike serenade on the bank of the lake; of carefully wrapped presents under a candle-lit tree; even of Christmas candy–all these memories faded away as he turned back and proclaimed into the darkening woods: "I'll see you again! Maybe tomorrow…or next week…or spring…or summer… ." He nodded his head in affirmation, the bill of his cap making comical arcs in front of his face as he proclaimed emphatically: "I'll see you again. You just wait."

Straightening himself on Spectrum's back, he leaned forward and gave his horse a topside hug–enduring a face-full of mane–and a few pats on the neck. Another faint whinny floated out of the woods. Sitting up straight and tall, he adjusted his cap, closed his eyes and gave his horse a brief squeeze with his legs. As Spectrum broke into a trot, Ted imagined bulging muscles pulsating under sleek, black hide. He imagined racing toward the pen on a steed that glided in an unrealistically smooth, graceful, stretching gait. "Go, boy, go!" he shouted, waving his arm in the air. Bent forward like a jockey, he perceived his dream as reality and rode his fantasy into the wind, harboring in his heart the secret of the wild horse. Ted Crockett grinned. He was happy…for now.

About the Author

Henry Petru was born into a farming family west of Corpus Christi, Texas, one of nine children. He participated in both farm work and farm play. One place of play was the area around the stock tank which supplied water for the livestock and fowl - including a horse. This tank area became the center of a story, this fictionalized narrative of events as Henry lived and dreamed them. In his teen years, he attended a religious seminary in San Antonio for over four years, returned to the farm and entered military service where he served for twenty-two years. During military service, he married a Japanese lady in Japan. Together, they raised two boys. Henry is now retired and lives in Austin, Texas.

Thank you for reading "Ted's Secret Dream: A Tale of Love and Adventure." I would appreciate you taking a few moments to write a review and send it to my publisher Positive Imaging, LLC at bill@positive-imaging.com . We welcome reviews and any comments. Thanks.

www.ingramcontent.com/pod-product-compliance
Lightning Source LLC
Chambersburg PA
CBHW070618310726
48982CB00001B/113

* 9 7 8 1 9 4 4 0 7 1 7 9 0 *